I0824523

MOVING AT THE SPEED OF TIME

A NOVEL

A TRAVELING SHOES PRESS BOOK

MOVING AT THE SPEED OF TIME

A NOVEL

JON CHRISTOPHER

TRAVELING SHOES PRESS
PO BOX 332
Pioneertown CA 92268

Moving At The Speed Of Time
ISBN# 978-1-7329205-6-9

First Hard Cover Edition | 2020
Edited by Jean-Paul L. Garnier
Book design by Jon Christopher

Dedicated to The Waldos

Ffftzoit!

CONTENTS

Prologue 11

1. **Location-34°08'05.8"N 116°18'54.6"W** 13
2. **Finding The Herb** 15
3. **Cosmic Ray Theory** 18
4. **The Routine** 21
5. **Time To Re-Up** 23
6. **The Waldos** 25
7. **Just Another Ex-Con** 27
8. **An Interesting Drug** 29
9. **Speed and Weed** 33
10. **Gift From Sirius** 36
11. **Smoke Break** 38
12. **Tripping** 40
13. **Bastard People** 44
14. **Making Art** 48
15. **Pee Test** 51
16. **The Fast** 53
17. **Two-Dog Plant** 57
18. **Big Winnings** 60
19. **The New Situation** 63
20. **On The Rocks** 66
21. **On The Road** 70

22. **Darlene** 73
23. **What If It's True?** 75
24. **It All Happened Before** 77
25. **Push On Through** 80
26. **Sadhus** 82
27. **Melanie** 84
28. **Viva Las Vegas** 86
29. **Freelandia** 88
30. **Living The Dream** 90
31. **Smoke Break** 94
32. **In The Hi-Desert** 96
33. **Giant Rock** 99
34. **Giant Rock, Postscript** 104
35. **Timeless Ones** 105
36. **Growing Pains** 108
37. **Naganites** 110
38. **Guy Fawkes Day** 112
39. **Augustus** 114
40. **Nagas For Real** 117
41. **Soul Searching** 119
42. **The Fire Dreamer** 121
43. **Educating Louie** 124
44. **Louie In Nagaland** 127
45. **Lung Issues** 129
46. **Bump In The Road** 132
47. **Bubba's Funk** 135
48. **Levels** 138
49. **Naga Bar** 141
50. **Heart Sick** 143
51. **Returning to Nagaland** 145

52. **Let's Go To Joshua Tree** 148
53. **A Tough Report** 151
54. **Peek Behind The Curtain** 153
55. **At The Drum Circle** 155
56. **House Hunting** 158
57. **Goldensnake** 162
58. **Open To The Public** 164
59. **Painting Nagas** 166
60. **Mysterious Forces** 168
61. **Just Carry On** 170
62. **Hi-Desert Dreaming** 172
63. **Home Inspection** 174
64. **New Moon Drum Circle** 176
65. **Men-in-Black** 179
66. **Run The Video** 181
67. **The Raid** 183
68. **After The Raid** 187
69. **The New Home** 189
70. **Visiting Bubba** 192
71. **Back To Washington** 197
72. **Dylan's Breakthrough** 200
73. **Smoke Break** 202
74. **The Road Back** 205
75. **Ffftzoit** 207

PROLOGUE

The muse of our story is a plant. The cannabis plant. Mary Jane. The Herb. Pot. Ganja. If I could, I'd make this a love song to the herb. But this isn't going to be a song, it's a novel, so I'm going to tell a story about marijuana instead. And if the story turns out to be about something else, at the least there will be the lingering smell of marijuana wafting from the pages. Right now I'm looking forward with little idea what kind of story is ahead. It's all quantum possibilities at this point.

I just got a new baggie of marijuana from my collective for the adventure ahead – an ounce of delicious looking buds of a strain called Girl Scout Cookies. I'm rolling up a big fat joint to smoke before we get this story going. I'm using the king size rolling papers. I'm thinking, if this baggie of pot doesn't help me kick out this story, nothing will.

I'm looking out over Joshua Tree National Park from our home in the hi-desert as I roll up this fatty. It's late in the afternoon, right around 4:20. The light is beautiful. A roadrunner is darting around the yard. He visits often, and I've named him Clack Clack. It's that magical time of the day so, as they say, "light 'em if you got 'em".

We'll be moving at the speed of time in this story, which is the only speed to go when you're good and stoned. Of course, that might leave you wondering how fast time is going. Maybe down the road we'll answer some questions about time, but then again, maybe we won't. Time will tell.

You might also be wondering, why this veneration of Mary Jane? What is so special about this herb that would inspire such devotion? Well, there are many reasons, as we'll discuss in the pages ahead but right now, in this prologue, it's because she's going to tell me a story, or help my intuition find the tale that's already out there in the collective consciousness.

You could say I am the consciousness that is turning the quantum possibilities of this moment into reality.

-1-

LOCATION-34°08'05.8"N 116°18'54.6"W

EPIGRAPH

I am consciousness having the experience of being me. You are consciousness having the experience of being you. We are made of the same cloud of dust, living in a world of illusions. We are energy, information, and all possibilities.

We live in a world where the extremes live together. We are all one consciousness but we live individual lives. We are connected but we are disconnected. We are held down by gravity but just enough to keep us from becoming weightless. We use light to see but need darkness to have contrast. The world appears solid but is made up of empty space. We know love is the answer but always prepare for war.

We demand explanations for the unexplainable. The Universe is full of mystery, enigmas and the unseen dimensions but we pretend that we know it all when we should marvel in childlike wonder. We are consciousness experiencing the wide diversity of life, the journey is meant to be mysterious.

Right now, the solar system is on a journey, flying through the galaxy at 514,000 mph. With the sun at the center of the solar system as we corkscrew our way through the galaxy at this crazy speed, it takes us around 230 million years to circle the Milky Way. At that speed, you could circle the equator of planet Earth in 2 minutes and 54 seconds.

Not only are we flying through space at this incredible speed but we are rising and descending from the galactic plane while we circumnavigate the galaxy. We are traveling through the Orion Spur right now, 25,000 light years from the center of the galaxy and 25,000 light years from the edge of the galaxy. The time is the present, the past, and a little bit into the future.

At this moment you and I are sitting at a stop light waiting for the light to change so we can pull out onto Highway 62, Twentynine Palms Highway, as it's known. I want to make sure you know where we are as we get started on this little story.

We're on our way to Dylan Winslow's house, a short drive away. We are having a conversation about where marijuana originally came from thousands of years ago. While we drive I'll share with you the legend of Bubba Shiki, the original discoverer of the marijuana plant.

-2-

FINDING THE HERB

Bubba Shiki was a round fellow. He had a round body and a pleasant round face with a long flowing beard and lengthy dreadlocks, which were piled up on top of his head. He lived with a group of spiritual seekers in the foothills of the Hindu Kush Mountains.

This was many thousands of years ago, so far back in time that we call it before the mists of time. To Bubba Shiki it was just a Tuesday afternoon. He had left their camp early that morning and planned to hike high up into the mountains on a personal spiritual retreat.

As Bubba was walking along the path formed by years of spiritual seekers hiking up the mountain, a sight caught his eyes off the side of the path. There was a beautiful green plant shimmering gently in the afternoon light. Bubba Shiki, who was in a spiritually seeking mindset, thought the plant was calling to him.

The plant had a sweet, yet earthy smell. It was covered with sticky flowers that glistened in the sunlight. Bubba picked a few of the flower buds and squeezed them. He was amazed at how sticky his fingers were and stuck his fingers in his mouth to lick them clean. *Hmmm. What an interesting flavor,* thought Bubba, and he popped a few flower buds in his mouth and slowly chewed them. *What a strange taste,* he thought. Bubba had never seen or heard of this plant before and he had hiked this trail many times. After a snack of flower buds Bubba continued on his hike. Nearby, unseen by Bubba Shiki, were two aliens, Nommos to be exact. They had put that plant there, now they wanted to see how this human would react to it.

The sun had moved a little across the sky when Bubba started to feel an odd sensation filling his body. He could feel it spreading with a strange comforting sensation. Then his mind started to race with ideas. New ideas flooded his thoughts. He started putting ideas together that had never fit together before and was amazed that he had missed such simple truths.

On the mountainside he sat down and looked out across the valleys below. It had never looked as beautiful as it did now. Bubba thought about the plant whose flowers he had eaten a short while earlier and made the connection. Once he made the connection he got back up on his feet and headed down the mountain, back to the plant.

Bubba Shiki collected as many flower buds as he could carry and headed back to camp. His feet and legs felt funny and he laughed as he walked unsteadily. He was feeling so good inside he thought he was going to burst. He couldn't wait to share his discovery with his fellow spiritual seekers.

Bubba burst into camp full of enthusiasm and gathered all his brothers and sisters. There was Baba Shiki, their leader, Ravi Shiki, Fred Shiki and sister Mellon Shiki. The Shikis greeted Bubba's enthusiasm with an enthusiasm of their own and they quickly devoured the buds he had brought home. And everyone had a great evening, except Mellon who seemed to be affected particularly strongly by the flowers and fell asleep.

The Shikis immediately adopted the plant into their budding religion. They called the plant Ganja and gathered seeds from the plant to start a crop. Over the next few years the Shikis became the first marijuana farmers and they learned much about the plant. Mellon discovered smoking it one day while cooking in the kitchen and showed everyone how burning Ganja got you high much quicker. Mellon did much better with smoking then she did with eating the plant.

Within a decade the Shikis were on their way to becoming a popular local religion. Already they had learned the difference between eating the herb and smoking it, how to make it into a drink and how to make hash. They wrapped their religious life in the clothing of the local popular religion and added marijuana to it. A successful combination for the Shikis. The Shikis said that the plant was the embodiment of Shiva and that Shiva had helped Bubba find the plant.

Within twenty years the farming operation grew into a full-sized religious center and the popularity of the herb spread. Soon wherever people traded goods there was usually someone selling the herb. The seeds of the plant were considered sacred and the plants were encouraged to produce as many seeds as possible.

Mellon Shiki was the first to discover how good it was to smoke seedless Ganja. Mellon had complained to Fred Shiki a number of times about what a pain it was to pick all the seeds out of the buds. The seeds were fine to munch on but smelled awful when smoked and sometimes exploded in your face.

Fred set about trying to solve the problem by isolating the females from the males as soon as possible and only growing a crop of female plants. To do this Fred built the first greenhouse for marijuana. Fred was surprised how well his solution worked. The buds were seedless and denser, thicker, stickier and had a much stronger high. Mellon loved the buds Fred produced and the practice of creating sinsemilla, or seedless marijuana, spread.

The rest is history, as they say. At least that's how the legend goes.

-3-

COSMIC RAY THEORY

My friend, Dylan Winslow, lived in Southern California, out in the Mojave desert, near the small town of Joshua Tree. Dylan loved the desert for many reasons, the wide open spaces, the sparse populations, the creative environment, but mostly because it was the hi-desert and there was a certain romance to it. It's the quintessential Southern California desert.

The hi-desert near Joshua Tree is a land full of life: from jack rabbits and ground squirrels to a variety of lizards, snakes and tortoises. There are large Yucca plants, Hedgehog Cactus, Jumping Cactus, Creosote bushes and of course, the Joshua trees. The Joshua trees stand around iconically wherever you look. It was the land of Gram Parsons, The Eagles and plenty of rock and roll history. It was where native shamanism met UFO culture in a world of mystical possibilities.

Dylan lived near Joshua Tree for seven years and watched the influx of new arrivals from Los Angeles with mixed emotions. Like most people who have lived anywhere for a while, he felt somewhat resistant to the new outsiders. But then, on the other hand, Dylan loved the hi-desert, and he wanted other people to love the hi-desert too. Hadn't Dylan been the new outsider at one point? That was before the newfound popularity of Joshua Tree National Park started to overwhelm the local infrastructure of restaurants and shops.

Dylan, an artist in his mid-fifties with dreadlocks halfway down his back, was sitting on his patio with his wife Melanie, or Mel for short. It was late June and the sun had warmed up everything to a nice 92 degrees. At least the humidity was only ten percent. The patio had a covering and they were sitting in the shade about to light up the first joint of the day.

Dylan and Mel lived on a five-acre parcel overlooking the Morongo Basin. The Morongo Basin is a vast hi-desert basin in the Mojave that stretches from Yucca Valley in the west, through Joshua Tree, to Twentynine Palms and Wonder Valley in the east. From where they were sitting they could watch the traffic of Highway 62 rolling in a steady stream down from Twentynine Palms, 20 miles away. Dylan was holding the joint in his hand ready to light up.

Today he still had a little herb left. It was a strain called Gorilla Glue #4 and he had rolled most of it up into the joint he was holding. Running out of pot meant Dylan was going to have to get some more – today. He didn't like to run out of smoking supplies.

Something about the smell and taste of Gorilla Glue #4 reminded Dylan of when he first started getting high, back in 1983. Back then he had gotten a strain called Skunk Buds from Humboldt, in Northern California. Skunk buds were the best. They were a beautiful light green, very sticky and smelled like a skunk, but in a good way.

The joint was beautifully rolled, perfectly aerated. Dylan always rolled his joints with a crutch at the end. For those who might not know, a crutch is a small piece of rolled-up cardstock that forms a little filter on the end of the joint. It keeps you from getting pieces of pot in your mouth, and you can smoke the joint down to the end without burning your fingers.

Dylan loved that first joint of the morning. He liked to wait until he finished his first cup of coffee, then he would roll up a joint and enjoy it with his second cup. By that time the sleepy cobwebs had evaporated from his mind and the effects of the first coffee were kicking in. He especially loved it when Mel joined him, like today.

Dylan was looking at his joint and absentmindedly thinking about how fast the solar system was flying through the galaxy. As he lit the joint, he started wondering about cosmic rays. What were the cosmic rays like in our part of the galaxy?

He held in the first few hits, holding them deep in his lungs and exhaling through his nose. A familiar feeling settled throughout his body. It never ceased to amaze Dylan how good pot made his body feel. You would think after nearly thirty-five years of smoking he would have gotten used to it, but no, it always hit him in a fresh way. He passed the joint to Mel, who took a little hit. Mel usually didn't need much to feel the effects of the herb.

There is a theory about cosmic rays and how they affect life on this planet. It has been suggested that we are going through a particularly bad section of the galaxy right now and the cosmic rays are causing chaos and destruction on our planet. These cosmic rays apparently interfere with our brains and how they process information. According to this theory, which we'll call the Cosmic Ray Theory, soon we'll move into a better section of the galaxy without these harmful cosmic rays and humankind will blossom once again into a Golden Age. As I said, it's only a theory.

-4-
THE ROUTINE

Dylan had a routine and it had to do with surviving depression.

Certain mornings Dylan woke up feeling ill. Dylan had severe depression, which often affected him in a physical way. Dylan would wake up feeling like he had the flu because of the depression. He felt like he didn't fit in his own skin properly and was nauseous. His mind would have a looping voice saying, "You're stupid, you suck, you piece of shit," over and over again. The looping voice usually had nothing to do with what was going on in Dylan's life or how he felt about himself. Dylan was used to waking up to an assault of depression; he had been doing this routine for years. And the routine included smoking pot, lots of it, if need be.

Dylan had been seeing psychiatrists and therapists for well over twenty years. During that time he had tried nearly every prescription medication for depression. Dylan had reached a point where he didn't want to try any new medications, and he was tired of talking to therapists. He had been on the same medication for the last few years and it, sort of, helped. None of the pharmaceutical medicine helped him much, and the side effects were usually worse than the depression.

The depressions were a regular event. Approximately every few weeks Dylan went through a cycle of depression, from feeling good, to feeling ill for a week and a half, then back to feeling good again. And then the cycle started all over.

What had become important to Dylan was surviving the illness. Anything that would relieve the symptoms without making the situation worse was welcomed. And pot was the thing that made Dylan feel right, normal. So Dylan smoked a lot of pot because feeling right was much better than feeling sick for more than half the month.

The first thing doctors asked Dylan when finding out about his depressions was if he was suicidal. Doctors have to ask these questions. No, Dylan always said, even if suicidal thoughts were assaulting his brain at that moment. Dylan called these suicidal thoughts “suicide attacks”. These came when the depression got really bad, he did his best to ignore them. Of course, it’s hard to ignore a voice in your head screaming that you need to die. But Dylan had learned to do that over the years. Ignore the depression, ignore the suicide attacks, smoke pot to get over the physical illness and quiet down the negative loops. Dylan knew the routine.

-5-

TIME TO RE-UP

It was time for Dylan to re-up on pot. Eventually every baggie comes to an end and so had Dylan's. Lately Dylan has been avoiding the drive to a collective in Palm Springs every time he ran out by using a local medical marijuana delivery service called Dream Queen.

Each time Dylan had pot delivered he thought back to the days before medical marijuana was legal: the waiting to get ahold of your dealer, the dry periods when you couldn't find any, dealers having only one kind of pot-usually crappy imported, Mexican weed.

Now Dylan could get an Indica if he needed, or a Sativa, or a hybrid. Now he could get pot in chocolates, buy a vape pen cartridge and get more Gorilla Glue #4 anytime during regular business hours. Chocolates, a cartridge and some more Gorilla Glue #4 were just what Dylan had in mind for today.

Dylan checked the menu online to make sure what he wanted was available and then called the service. Dream Queen was run by a nice, middle-aged couple named Cathy and Paul. They really have a place in their hearts for medical patients. Cathy and Dylan have had long talks about it.

Cathy told Dylan she'd send Alex right away. Dylan liked Alex. Alex wore crystals and was a kind desert hippie. Every time Alex delivered he was wearing a different crystal around his neck on a leather cord. Dylan asked him about the crystals once and Alex had given a thorough run down on what the crystal he was wearing did for him.

Alex showed up about thirty minutes later with Dylan's herb request nicely packaged in a prescription bag. Dylan used his ATM card to pay for the purchase. It was all so easy, just the way God intended it.

-6-

THE WALDOS

Time for a smoke break, the first of many smoke breaks ahead. I just lit up a joint of Girl Scout Cookies. In a moment we'll continue with our story, but first let me tell you about the Waldos.

In the laid-back town of San Rafael, California, in the early 1970s there were a group of five laid-back guys that hung out on a low wall at their high school. They were called the Waldos. The Waldos were a good-natured bunch of guys, football players and cross-country runners. They liked to goof around, do imitations of people they knew and make funny noises like "Eyot" and "Ffftzoit", which should be said after taking a hit off of a joint.

One day they were given a map to a secret pot garden on Pt. Reyes Peninsula. The owners of the map, a group of U.S. Coast Guards, had grown the marijuana but now they were afraid their commanding officer was on to them, so they abandoned the garden just when it was ready to be harvested. One of the Coast Guards had given the map to his younger brother Bill, who gave the map to the Waldos.

The Waldos decided to meet after school by the statue of

Louis Pasteur at 4:20 to go search for the secret garden. All day long, as the Waldos passed each other in the halls, they would say “Louis 420”. It was their inside code.

After school, at 4:20, they got high by the Louis Pasteur statue, piled into a 1966 Chevy Safari and went off on their quest. They didn’t find the garden that day but they continued their search for months. After a little while “Louis” was dropped from the saying and the secret greeting of “420” continued.

The Waldos got to know the Grateful Dead through both Waldo Dave’s older brother and Waldo Mark’s father, who rented rehearsal space to the band. The Grateful Dead and their friends picked up the 420 code and passed it on. 420 is now an international code word for pot smoking and April 20th has become an international holiday for pot smokers. Every day pot smokers around the world light up when it’s 4:20 in the afternoon, in solidarity.

Good job Waldos.

-7-
JUST ANOTHER EX-CON

It didn't matter how long of a shower Louie Gilder took, he couldn't get the smell of prison off of him. He had been out for five years now, living a straight life, and he still smelled like prison to himself, and he was sure everyone else could smell it too. To compensate, Louie took long showers, and wore way too much cologne.

Louie got busted fifteen years ago for growing the herb, close to 200 plants. Louie was a different person fifteen years ago. He had done his time and gotten out on good behavior. The police had taken everything he had, his house, his land, his cars and his girlfriend, Leslie. She had turned state's evidence, gotten off lightly and never spoke to Louie again. When Louie got out he had nothing left but the smell of prison.

For six months Louie lived in a half-way house and worked jobs the state provided, which were mostly menial. Eventually Louie got a small studio apartment of his own. Louie called it his cell.

Louie kept clean and sober, just like his parole required. He met with his parole officer regularly and took his pee test when required, always striving to regain a normal person's life.

After five years Louie's parole was over and he was just another ex-convict, hanging on to the fringes of society. Louie had a couple street friends but both of them were doing time at the moment. Other than that he had no connections and liked to keep it that way. He hadn't smoked pot in fifteen years and he planned to keep it that way too.

Louie often felt like something was missing in his life. He wasn't sure what it was, but there was a hole in his heart that nothing could fill. He thought that maybe it had something to do with his job. Maybe he needed a different kind of work.

Louie was a natural green thumb and got a job working for a landscaping company. It was the only work he could find. Every job he applied for turned him down except for the Mexican landscaping company he now worked for called Jesus & Jesus. Louie was convinced that the convict smell was keeping him for getting something different.

Not that Louie needed another line of work, he fit right in with the landscaping crew and quickly learned Spanish on the job. He got up every morning at three to meditate and pray and met the landscaping crew at five. The crew usually worked until around three or whenever the day's work was done. Everyone on the crew had a nickname and Louie's was "Oro" because of his golden touch with plants.

Some people have suggested that the reason certain people have so-called green thumbs is because they vibrate at the same level as plants. They vibrate at a level of empathy that causes extra health in the plants around them. Whatever the truth might be, it is true that certain individuals are better at growing plants than others. Plants, it seems, don't care if you've been in prison. They do care if you're a compassionate soul and Louie had a compassionate soul.

-8-

AN INTERESTING DRUG

Dylan went through a divorce a number of years ago. He is still good friends with his ex-wife, Marie. They were married for twenty years and didn't have any kids together. Dylan and Marie Kovak had met when they were young, when they both were mods.

Mods were a youth movement, a sub-culture, in the early 1980s that looked to the mods of the early 1960s for inspiration. They rode Vespa scooters, wore early 1960s styled suits and clothing, took lots of speed and danced the nights away at clubs to soul, ska, and power-pop music.

Being a mod was all about going fast. Zipping around on their scooters decked out in mirrors and lights. Dancing late into the night at clubs, hanging out at Denny's at 3:00AM drinking coffee and going, always going. This going and going usually meant taking lots of speed pills: purple hearts, Christmas trees, or white cross tops.

Dylan started taking speed as soon as he began hanging out with mods. He found a great connection for speed pills and started dealing. It paid for all the little expenses like clove cigarettes, scooter gas, clothes, records, and clubs.

Dylan had been dealing speed for nearly a year when one of his customers offered to trade some pot for a handful of pills. Dylan had only smoked pot once in his life, several years earlier, and it hadn't done anything for him. Dylan didn't really want to make the trade but did anyway.

Dylan carried the pot around with him for several weeks until he almost forgot about it. One day he was at a record store, Pier Records in Newport Beach, and he noticed they had a head shop in the back. It was the first one he had ever been in. He studied the case of pipes. The variety seemed endless. Dylan picked out a nice little wooden pipe, bought it and left.

Dylan worked at a run-down movie theater in Costa Mesa. He was an usher and sometimes worked behind the snack bar. He was the guy who walked through with a flashlight in the middle of the movie. Dylan's manager was one of his speed customers, a nice guy named Matt. Matt was also a pot smoker and one evening Dylan suggested they smoke some of his pot. Matt motioned to the manager's office.

Once they were in the office Dylan got out his pot and his new pipe. Matt took a look at his pipe.

"Nice little pipe, do you have any screens?" asked Matt.

"Screens? What are screens?" replied Dylan.

"They are little mesh circles you put in the bowl of the pipe, so you don't inhale ashes."

"No, I don't have any screens," Dylan was confused.

Matt really didn't want to get stoned at work. He was planning on just taking a small toke, so he was relieved Dylan didn't have any screens.

"Well, I guess that's that," said Matt, moving towards the door, "get some screens at Pier Records next time you're there."

Dylan went and bought screens the next evening. He didn't work for a couple of days, so he called up his friend Sue and asked her if she wanted to get stoned. "Hell yeah" was her response. Sue was an enthusiastic pot smoker. That night she taught him the basics of getting high: how to pack a bowl, how to take a hit, how to hold it in and how to wait to feel the effects.

Dylan and Sue were good friends but there was nothing romantic between them. Sue had a boyfriend who lived in Newport Beach. He had broken his knee and was in a full leg cast, so he didn't get around much. Sue lived with two prostitutes, or call girls as they liked to call themselves, both heroin addicts.

Dylan got high for his first time watching the Dave Letterman Show. After a few hits from the pipe Dylan felt a strange comfortable feeling spread through his body. He hadn't realized how uncomfortable his body had been until this new feeling settled in him.

Dave Letterman started to change and became a cartoon, or looked like a cartoon. Dylan got lost in thought for a while staring at the television set, amazed at the way Dave Letterman had transformed.

Now this is an interesting drug, thought Dylan.

The marijuana took the edge off the speed. Dylan noticed this effect right away. This was about the most interesting drug Dylan had encountered, so far.

Sue, Dylan and the two call girls, who weren't working that night, hung out and watched television for several hours. It was the most engaging TV Dylan had ever watched. Around two in the morning Dylan felt he was straight enough to drive home, twenty-five miles away.

The adventure driving home was like no other scooter ride he had experienced. Dylan was amazed how slow he was driving while it seemed so fast. The drive took so long but Dylan had never enjoyed the ride more. Luckily he didn't encounter any police officers on the way home and nothing ruined Dylan's stoned vibe.

When Dylan got home to the house he lived at with his parents in Irvine, he got out his new pipe and packed a bowl the way Sue had showed him. He sat out front of his parent's house on his scooter and took several hits. Then he smoked a couple cigarettes. The neighborhood was still and quiet at 3AM.

Dylan couldn't remember a time he felt as good as he did at that moment. Dylan had found his drug of choice. Even more than speed, cannabis felt good. It made his body feel "right". It made his mind race with ideas, like deciding to paint his scooter a new color the next day, for instance.

-9-

SPEED AND WEED

Dylan and Marie started dating soon after he began smoking pot. You could call it dating, but it was more like hanging out together. Marie loved to smoke pot, but she didn't care much for Dylan when he was on speed. When he was on speed he talked too much about nothing. Sometimes he was agitated and sometimes he was paranoid. When he got stoned he slowed down and thought more about what he wanted to say. The stoned version of Dylan was much more interesting and laid back.

After Dylan had been smoking pot for several months he started to wonder about his speed intake. The paranoia was starting to bother him. He had become dependent on speed to get anything done. Marie, who took speed every once in a while, was more interested in coke than speed pills and preferred marijuana to both coke and speed.

When Dylan brought up the idea of quitting speed Marie encouraged him. So he did one day, he quit cold turkey. And then he got sick, very sick.

Dylan hadn't been expecting withdrawal symptoms. For several days he laid in his room, sweating and aching, just trying to survive. At night, when everyone else was in bed, he would make his way down the hall, through his dad's study to the balcony. There he would smoke a bowl of marijuana and feel better for a while. Smoking the herb helped Dylan get through the sickness, further endearing marijuana to his heart.

In the months after Dylan quit taking speed he decided to quit selling too. He told his customers he was going to quit and tried to help some of his friends get stocked up. Dylan knew withdrawal sucked. He encouraged his friends to start smoking pot instead. He made it a point to get people stoned when they asked him for speed pills. Dylan notched his pipe each time he got someone high for the first time. His pipe had over seventy notches before it was lost.

Soon a small subset of mods had turned to marijuana. At one particular night club in Los Angeles, the Lhasa Club, they could smoke pot freely. When they took a break from dancing, they would retire to a side room where they would form a small circle of dedicated pot smokers to pass around the pipe. Anyone could sit in on a session if they had pot to contribute, sitting in on a session was considered a pretty cool thing to do.

Marie really liked the changes in Dylan since he quit taking speed. It took months for the paranoia to go away but eventually all the effects from his speed intake faded. Cannabis was definitely a part of his healing process.

Dylan spontaneously proposed to Marie one night. You can blame it on the especially strong marijuana they were smoking, some Thai sticks. Thai sticks were these delicious Thai buds that were wrapped around a bamboo stick, then tied with red thread, and cured for weeks to supreme fineness. Sometimes the Thai sticks were dipped in hash oil to make them extra potent. These were the kind of Thai sticks Dylan and Marie were smoking. Marie said yes right away. They spent the rest of the evening talking about when, where, and how to get married.

They got married six months later at a little church, a

marriage chapel, on the Palos Verde Peninsula, just north of San Pedro. Marie's dad, Frank, paid for the wedding. Frank Kovac was some big wig for an oil company. I actually have no idea want he did at his job but it paid well.

-10-
GIFT FROM SIRIUS

There are so many cultures since the days of Bubba Shiki that have made cannabis their own. Why? Because cannabis is a wondrous plant. It's the original do-all plant. You can do just about anything with cannabis. It has the strongest fibers and can be woven into incredibly durable clothing. The seeds are amazingly nutritious. The flowers get you high. And if you're into plastics, the cellulose of the cannabis plant can be broken down and used in any way you can use plastics. It makes great paper. It's over the top when it comes to useful.

Cannabis is such an amazing, all-purpose plant a person would naturally wonder where it came from, historically speaking. The best historical evidence suggests that humankind has used this plant for at least 12,000 years. Many Native American tribes have stories and traditions that say that the Star People from Sirius brought this plant to Earth, as a gift. If that's the truth, then it was a great gift indeed.

The Dogon tribe of Mali Africa call marijuana the "two-dog plant". They say it was brought to them by the Nommos from Sirius, the Dog Star. As it turns out, these are the same Nommos that planted the cannabis plant which Bubba Shiki found. They say the Nommos brought them the plant in 3200 BC.

Here's a bit of information about Sirius, the Dog Star. The Dog Star is actually made up of two stars. Sirius A and Sirius B are a binary star system and appear as a single bright star in the Canis Major constellation. Only Sirius A is visible with the naked eye, you need a telescope to see Sirius B. But, amazingly, the Dogon knew long ago about Sirius B because Star People, the Nommos, an amphibious race of creatures who brought them the two-dog plant, told them about it. There is a third star in the Sirius system, a small red star we call Sirius C, around which orbits the Nommos' planet. The Dogon knew about this planet too, but we only discovered it with our powerful telescopes in 1995.

Of course, we cannot be sure if the Dogon were truly visited by the Nommos. But considering that they have built their entire culture around the arrival of the Nommos, the two-dog plant and the Sirius star system, the Dogon get my benefit of the doubt.

And what about the numerous Native American tribes, do they get the benefit of the doubt too? I think so. We are so arrogant in Western Culture with regards to the deeply held beliefs of our fellow humans. We are condescending without even trying. We call their beliefs, which they have held for so long, *just* myths, stories and legends. Maybe their stories aren't just myths but a way of telling about real events.

Maybe our world is larger and stranger than we care to imagine. Maybe history is a much deeper, longer and richer story then we've been led to believe. Maybe we live in a galaxy where Nommos live on a planet in the Sirius star system and brought us the amazing plant, cannabis.

-11-

SMOKE BREAK

I've rolled up another nice fat joint to smoke before the next chapter starts. I'm really loving this strain, Girl Scout Cookies. Here's the description from a website:

"Girl Scout Cookies, or GSC, is an OG Kush and Durban Poison hybrid cross. With a sweet and earthy aroma, Girl Scout Cookies launches you to euphoria's top floor where full-body relaxation meets a time-bending cerebral space. A little goes a long way with this hybrid."

I like euphoria's top floor as well as full-body relaxation meeting time-bending cerebral space. It might not be for everyone, but it works for me.

Here is one of the beautiful things about cannabis - it comes in so many varieties, or strains, but when you get down to it, according to our current understanding, there are three basic types of pot:

You can get a pot that's great for pain management, and for helping with relaxing, anxiety, and sleeping, a totally mellow herb. This type of herb is called Indica, and includes strains like Hindu Kush, Granddaddy Purple, Northern Lights and Blueberry. Indica plants tend to be shorter and have broader leaves then their sisters.

At the other end of the marijuana spectrum is the Sativa plants. The Sativa buzz is considerably more active and uplifting then the Indica buzz. Some people call Sativa the day time herb. Some classic Sativa strains include Sour Diesel, Green Crack, Durban Poison and the old school Maui Wowie. Sativas tend to be taller plants and have long thin leaves.

Occupying the middle ground is a wide number of strains called Hybrids and include Girl Scout Cookies, Gorilla Glue #4, OG Kush, Pineapple Express and about 1,180 other different strains. The effects found in the hybrids vary widely. Dylan would recommend asking the budtenders at your collective about any hybrids you're interested in trying. Those budtenders can be quite knowledgeable.

Ffftzoit.

-12-
TRIPPING

Marie was a year younger than Dylan but much older in many ways. She was of Hungarian descent and what people call an old soul. She had been a mod for a while because her friends from school had been mods. Once she met Dylan she started to lose her interest in the whole mod thing. She was more interested in taking acid now. She had a best friend named Marcella Richards, who loved everything about the Rolling Stones, especially the fact that she had the same last name as Keith Richards. Marcella also loved taking acid and smoking pot.

While Marie had a full figure with large breasts, Marcella was flat as a board, tall and skinny. Marie liked to keep her blonde hair cut short and spiky while Marcella let her brown hair grow long and didn't pay much attention to it. Marie liked John Lennon and Marcella loved Keith Richards.

Marcella didn't care to much for Marie's choice in men, and kind of wished Dylan would just go away. She was civil to him in person, but preferred it when he wasn't around. At least until they all took acid one weekend.

After they got married, Dylan and Marie had moved to an apartment in Costa Mesa, just off of Harbor Boulevard. They had a brief honeymoon to Northern California, a road trip so they could bring plenty of pot with them. They traveled all they way to Eureka and back home to Orange Country, driving on the coast whenever possible. They got high often, and had many long conversations while they slowly cruised the back roads. Marie did most of the driving while Dylan rode shotgun, map in hand, navigating and rolling joints. It was during this trip, while smoking a fatty in the Redwoods that Marie convinced Dylan to try acid when they got back home. Dylan was nervous about the idea. He had heard a lot of scary stories about acid back when he was in high school.

It was a pleasant Saturday morning when Marcella came by with hits of LSD for the three of them. Marcella had taken acid at least twenty times and was going to lead the trip, at least that was the plan beforehand. She had brought six hits of blotter acid, just in case someone else showed up. The blotter acid was pretty good stuff. It had little pictures of Felix the Cat all over it.

"Here's to Felix' magic bags of tricks," said Marcella as they put the tabs of acid on their tongues.

They took acid around noon, and smoked a joint while they waited for it to kick in, which took about an hour.

Marcella kept going into the bathroom to look in the mirror. She said that's how she knew it was taking effect, her face in the mirror gets a bit funny.

"Funny how?" Dylan wanted to know.

"Don't know how to describe it. Lopsided, I guess," she said, "You'll see in a little bit."

Dylan was looking forward to seeing what a hallucination looked like. He had done a bunch of research beforehand and felt he was ready for whatever happened.

What happened was the walls and the ceiling started to shift and move. They didn't seem to be touching. Dylan noticed it as a subtle effect at first and then the shifting and sliding increased. Dylan started laughing and couldn't stop. Then Marie started laughing, then Marcella. Dylan rolled off of the sofa, landed on his back and kicked his legs in the air, still laughing. Something was definitely happening and it felt right, like the perfect thing to be happening at that moment.

Dylan sat up and looked at Marie and Marcella and said, "Yes, this is perfect". Marie and Marcella felt the exact same way. What followed was a thorough examination of the apartment. Furniture was rearranged. Closets were investigated. For three hours the trio explored the place. Marie got the idea while they were sitting on the floor of the spare bedroom that they should drive to Balboa Island to see the sunset.

The drive to Balboa Island was amazingly easy. It was like the car drove itself. Marie had been so involved in the conversation she didn't remember driving the car. Marcella rolled around in the back seat as they went around corners. Dylan, who sat in the passenger seat, rolled up several joints for walking around the small island packed with expensive homes and docks with boats and yachts.

The three of them took a half hour to leave the car. Meanwhile they smoked another fatty, which they didn't really feel but it seemed like a good thing to do before getting out and continuing their adventure. They took several hours to make the twenty minute walk around Balboa Island. Everywhere seemed like a great place to sit, have a cigarette and talk about stuff. They took the ferry across the Newport Harbor to Balboa Peninsula and wandered the arcades for a while. They walked out to the beach and watched the sunset. It was beautiful, they all agreed.

It was dark when they took the ferry back to the Island and tried to find their car. They had been on their trip for eight hours when they finally found it, the acid was still going strong. The group had bonded as adventurers on a quest, and driving back to the apartment was the next feat that must be performed.

Marie paid a little more attention on the way home, mostly her instincts as an excellent driver took over. The lights were much more distracting driving at night, everything had trails of light coming off of them. They got home safely and went up to the apartment.

The rest of the trip, the next three hours, was spent hanging out and watching videos on MTV. Marcella spent the night on the sofa, smoking pot and cigarettes until dawn, watching late, late night movies, while both Dylan and Marie had a sound sleep. Now Marcella felt better about her best friend marrying Dylan.

Dylan and Marie woke up sore the next morning. It seemed like every muscle ached from overuse. Marcella, who was expecting to be tired the day after taking acid, wasn't surprised. They went to Denny's for breakfast and came home ready to take a long afternoon nap, which they did.

-13-

BASTARD PEOPLE

LSD was made illegal in California in 1966. Marijuana was made illegal in 1937. In 1984, when Dylan, Marie and Marcella were taking acid, the War on Drugs was just starting to ramp up, again. Nancy Reagan, the First Lady, had latched onto the *Just Say No* campaign.

One story has it that Nancy Reagan needed some good PR after the White House China snafu. Nancy Reagan spent close to $200,000 on new China for the White House when the Reagans moved there in 1981. There was a huge backlash against Nancy and people took to calling her Queen Nancy. Her first attempt at public image rehabilitation was to announce that she was going to focus on the Foster Grandparents Program. That went nowhere. So the PR machine went back to work, and it paid off.

Next we had Nancy at a public school in 1982 when a child asked her what to do if someone tries to sell her drugs. Nancy, quick on her feet, and well-prepared, said, "Just Say No". This slogan, the product of a drug-resistance program establish in 1970, became Nancy Reagan's theme song for the rest of the Reagan administration. Drug use increased during the administration and drug-related arrests went through the roof as the country suffered through an insanity called the War of Drugs. Meanwhile the CIA was shipping massive amounts of cocaine into the United States, to sell to the ever-growing street gangs, to support their covert overseas wars. The hypocrisy of the government throughout the War on Drugs has been ridiculous, but then again, the government's long fight against drugs has always been of dubious value morally, financially, and socially.

Take the herb, for instance. In the 1800s cannabis was included as an ingredient in many medications. Pharmacist couldn't imagine not having cannabis extract in their cabinet of medicines. But then Mexico had a revolution and numerous immigrants from Mexico flooded into the southern states. These new immigrants brought with them the habit of smoking cannabis recreationally, which they called marijuana.

There was a huge racist backlash against the new immigrants, as is the habit of our country. Into the racist backlash stepped Harry J. Anslinger, the first head of the Federal Bureau of Narcotics. Looking for something to prohibit once alcohol prohibition ended in the early 1930s, Anslinger choose marijuana. Using numerous racist lies Anslinger built a campaign to make marijuana illegal. Black men smoking pot, and seducing white women. Marijuana crazed Mexicans killing their families with axes. White women smoking pot and having sex with non-white men. The stories went on and on.

The Hearst Newspapers were only too happy to further this anti-marijuana campaign. First of all, William Randolph Hearst hated the Mexicans since they had seized hundreds of acres of timberland he owned in Mexico during the revolution. Second of all, Hearst still owned hundreds of acres of forests in the United States which he planned to turn into newsprint and didn't like the competition from cannabis, also known as hemp. Hemp is a non-psychoactive cannabis plant, not any good for smoking but great for industrial purposes.

Hemp makes fantastic paper and is a renewable resource. The only problem with hemp in our industrialized world was the immense amount of effort it took to harvest, but that was about to change. Just before marijuana was made illegal using the Stamp Act of 1937, a machine had been invented that immensely simplified the harvest process and set the stage for hemp marijuana to become the next billion dollar crop.

When the Stamp Act passed in early 1937 it instantly became ridiculously expensive to grow and harvest hemp. Competition for both Hearst and the DuPont Corporation were squashed with one new law. The DuPont Corporation specialized in plastics, and had invested heavily in petroleum-based plastic. Hemp-based plastic was unneeded competition for their new products. I'm not saying there was any conspiracy, but I'm not saying there wasn't one.

Once marijuana was made illegal Anslinger could begin to justify ever growing budgets for his new bureau. It became easier to fill the jails with brown and black bodies. Police found new reasons to harass otherwise law-abiding citizens. Hearst continued to turn trees into newsprint and DuPont's stocks grew.

Over time reality caught up with the stories of marijuana-fueled murders. People began to realize that marijuana was the same drug they had been using for years called cannabis. So new lies were invented. Marijuana was a gateway drug, they said. Once a person started smoking marijuana they would inevitably graduate to shooting heroin, as sure as night followed day, they said. This is, of course, ridiculous. But that didn't stop this lie from horrifying the ignorant and law-abiding populace.

And so the battle against marijuana, based on lies, continued for years, only to be ramped up by the crooked President, Richard M. Nixon. Nixon was responsible for a whole new wave of marijuana persecution by introducing the "Schedules" for drugs, placing marijuana on the most restricted level,

Schedule I. Ronald Reagan carried on Nixon's War on Drugs and pushed it to new extremes. Many people heap praise on Ronald Reagan but I have nothing but scorn for the Reagans, both Ronnie and Nancy. They are directly responsible for ruining countless lives with their evil War on Drugs. Selfish, bastard people. Same with Henry J. Anslinger. Same with William Randolph Hearst. Bastard people.

-14-
MAKING ART

Dylan and Marie took acid a bunch of times over the next year and became skilled at navigating the world while baking hard on LSD. After a while though, Dylan started to get tired with how long the trips lasted. After three hours into a trip he would wish the acid would wear off, but it doesn't for ten to twelve hours. One night Marie brought up the fact she was getting tired of taking acid and Dylan, greatly relieved, told her that was how he was feeling too. And so, with that, the period of experimenting with LSD was over.

That's how it often goes with drug experimentation. A person tries a drug for a while, and then they're done with it. They learn all they can from that drug and move on to new things. Of course, some drugs are more dangerous to experiment with than others.

Meanwhile, Dylan and Marie continued to love the herb. It was such a pleasant way to relax, in spite of the increasingly hysterical political and social climate.

Marie was going to school at the University of California in Irvine, working towards a degree in Education Administration. Dylan was working an endless number of nowhere jobs. Currently he was driving a truck for an auto parts supplier, delivering auto parts to car dealerships and motor home repair shops. Marie's dad was helping to supplement their income by paying their rent, at least while Marie was in school.

Marie had introduced Dylan to art several years earlier by taking him to a Pop Art exhibit at the Temporary Contemporary Art Museum in Los Angeles. Dylan had never seen real art up close before. The show included Lichtenstein, Warhol, Rauschenberg and many others. Dylan was inspired and started to experiment with painting, using the spare bedroom as his studio. For several years he muddled around, making messes on the canvas, but not much more. In his opinion his paintings looked like crap. Marie continued to encourage him.

Dylan liked doing drawings with charcoal, and mostly drew hands, which is what he had learned to do in a drawing class at Orange Coast College several years earlier. Hands... hands holding candles, hands holding crosses, hands with trees growing out of the palms, and he could draw penises. Dylan was particularly good at drawing penises, but his paintings looked awful and amateurish, and he knew it. Nothing he did looked like art.

One day Dylan got the idea to photocopy his cigarette pack while at the copy store. The pack was empty so he smashed it flat and made a photocopy. The resulting black and white image was the first interesting image Dylan had ever created. He looked at the photocopy for a while wondering what to do with it. And then he had a flash of inspiration.

Dylan bought some gloss medium at the art store next door and went back to the copy store. He blew up the photocopy on numerous pieces of paper until the resulting image was the size of a large canvas. That night he pasted the blown-up photocopies of the smashed cigarette pack onto a canvas with the gloss medium. He painted the background black and after a couple of hours he was done. He stepped back to admire his work.

"Now, that is cool," said Marie coming through the door of the studio bringing Dylan a cup of coffee.

Dylan was lost in thought, kind of amazed that the piece he was looking at had been created by his own hands.

"What?" asked Dylan.

"That looks really cool," said Marie.

"Thanks," replied Dylan.

Dylan sipped on the coffee and they stared at the smashed cigarette pack.

"You know, this canvas looks like art," said Marie after a while.

"That's what I was thinking," replied Dylan.

-15-

PEE TEST

Dylan did a number of collage paintings of smashed cigarette packs. After a few months he had twenty-five canvases ready for a show, if he could find a gallery that would show his work. Meanwhile, Marie was getting close to graduation and had already lined up a job interview as an administrator for the Irvine School District. Unfortunately the job required Marie to get a urine test.

This was a new thing, having to take a pee test to get a job. Dylan was incensed about the whole idea. Marie, who wasn't looking forward to not smoking pot for a while, was still okay with the idea. Marie and Dylan argued late into the night about it one evening.

Dylan was sometimes argumentative, especially when something upset his freedom-loving principles. Marie couldn't care less either way but Dylan wouldn't let it alone. Eventually Marie asked Dylan to kindly shut the fuck up. Dylan, completely fired up, grabbed his keys, stormed out of the house and drove around for a couple hours until he cooled off.

Dylan had been on a downward spiral for a few weeks and even though he didn't know what was going on, a severe depression was settling in on him. The pee test situation had pushed against his already fraying nerves.

All that Dylan knew was that he didn't feel like painting and his brain seemed like a clouded mess.

"I feel like I've run out of gas," he had said to Marie one evening a few days earlier.

When Dylan smoked the herb he felt better for a while but still the world was turning into a big drag. Some days his brain seemed to be screaming but he didn't know what it was screaming about. One morning he found himself thinking about ending it all. Everything in him suggested that killing himself was the best course of action. His brain fixated on the idea of suicide and for several days it was all he could think about. He tried to think of how he could do this in the least painful way possible. Dylan kept these thoughts to himself. If he told anyone, he figured, they'd try and stop him. After several days the suicidal thoughts started to fade and Dylan wondered what he had just been through. Dylan had been through periods like this before but never with the suicidal thoughts.

-16-
THE FAST

Marie got the job with the Irvine School District and Dylan continued to paint and soon nearly ten years had gone by. They were now living in a house in Irvine. Dylan had turned the garage into a studio and had become a prolific painter. He had been in art shows from Los Angeles to New York and his work was selling well. His collage painting style had opened up a whole world of image possibilities and he painted series after series of everyday objects in his evolving neo-Pop style.

By this time Dylan had also gone through numerous cycles of depression with suicidal thoughts. When he was in his late twenties he had a complete breakdown and was hospitalized for several weeks. He hadn't tried to kill himself but he was making plans. Marie was freaked out by the experience. The doctors diagnosed Dylan as having bipolar disorder with severe depression. Dylan was put on an anti-depression medicine that made him feel like a zombie. For months Dylan didn't paint. The medication seem to suck all the creativity out of him. His doctor switched medication and it made him gain thirty pounds. He switched medications again and this time the doctor added a mood stabilizer. He had headaches all the time. And so it went, new medication, new side effects, change medication, repeat. Each change of medication took a month or more and then several months before the new drug could be evaluated. Dylan came to the conclusion, after years of this, that the medications were worse than the illness.

What did help? Marijuana, of course. Through the whole trial and error with medications Dylan continued to smoke the herb when the depression got bad, to relieve the symptoms. Dylan didn't tell his doctor about the herb smoking because he didn't want to be forced into a drug-rehab program. That had happened to a friend of his who had tried to be honest with his doctor about how smoking the herb helped him.

In 1995 Dylan decided to take a break from smoking pot. He had been smoking pot for twelve years. *What if smoking pot is causing my depressions,* he wondered? Dylan decided on taking a five hundred day break, he called it a fast, to see how his body would react. Marie seldom smoked pot anymore and the idea of Dylan taking a break from smoking pot sounded great. Dylan told Marie he was going to meditate on compassion for the five hundred days.

"I'm so tired of the War of Drugs," Dylan had complained to Marie one day, "nobody cares about their neighbor anymore, no one has any compassion for the marijuana user."

Dylan smoked his last pot for a long time on Memorial Day weekend, 1995.

It wasn't easy quitting pot, especially for someone who had smoked it almost daily for twelve years. It took Dylan over a month before he started to get used to not smoking pot whenever he felt like it. Painting was awkward and strange. He had never painted without being stoned. He was used to taking pot smoking breaks while he worked on a painting. It was a habit. Over the next several months Dylan became acutely aware of how habitual his marijuana use had become. Dylan gave up trying to paint for a while and tried writing. He bought a computer with a word processor program on it. Dylan spent several hours every day at the computer trying to get his thoughts in order. He wrote a lot about compassion and about the War on Drugs.

Five hundred days seemed to take forever. Finally, in October of 1996, Dylan's fast came to an end. During the five hundred days the depressions had still come and gone, just like before. The lack of pot didn't make the depressions go away, it just made them harder to live through. Several times Dylan thought he might need to go back in the hospital again. Because of the fast Marie had realized how helpful marijuana was for Dylan and was looking forward to him smoking again.

Dylan and Marie took a small vacation to San Francisco to celebrate the end of Dylan's fast. They stayed in a little hotel on a side street near Chinatown. Dylan contacted his old pot dealer before the trip and got an eighth of some powerful herb called The Chronic.

On the morning of the day Dylan broke his fast he sat by the window of their hotel room and packed a bowl of The Chronic into a brand new pipe. The music of the Gipsy Kings was playing from a nearby apartment. Dylan took a big hit and held it in. *Oh yum,* he thought.

The old, familiar feeling spread through his system as the THC hit his bloodstream and was carried to the farthest reaches of his body. Then the herb hit his brain. Oh, it was good to be back. He savored the moment.

He handed the pipe to Marie and she took a hit, held it in, and blew it out the window.

The next few hours were a stoned out bliss as he and Marie wandered around Chinatown taking numerous photos. Everything looked like a photo opportunity. When they got back to the hotel room Dylan made several drawings of souvenirs they had bought. It felt good to draw again.

One month later, Proposition 215, The Compassionate Use Act, passed in California and medical marijuana became a legal reality for the first time in decades. Dylan wondered for years if his fast for five hundred days had helped in the passage of Proposition 215. It's a strange world, and who knows, after all he had been meditating for five hundred days on compassion. They say meditations and intentions go a long way and can even alter the collective consciousness in profound way.

-17-
TWO-DOG PLANT

Time to roll-up a fatty of this divine Girl Scout Cookies herb and take another smoke break.

I've been thinking about the Dogon tribe in Mali, Africa. I mean, what if their picture of the Universe is accurate? What if marijuana really did come from the Nommos, the Star People? What if cannabis really is an alien plant? What if there are humans around the galaxy smoking pot?

Let's consider a few items. Cannabis is the only plant that produces cannabinoids. Cannabinoids are chemical compounds like THC and CBD which are responsible for the effects of marijuana. Humans produce cannabinoids naturally too and have built in receptors for cannabinoids in their brains. We are built to ingest marijuana.

Cannabis is one of the few plants that has distinctly different sexes. Cannabis grows as either a male or a female plant. A cannabis plant can sometimes be a hermaphrodite and produce both male and female flowers but it's not the norm. While there are other plants that have distinctly different sexes, most don't.

Before 12,000 years ago there is no record of cannabis,

anywhere on the planet. It's not in the fossil record. It just shows up all of a sudden, fully developed. Ready to help humankind in numerous ways.

The Dogon have based their culture on Sirius and the two-dog plant, a most interesting name when you consider the words that make up the single word cannabis. "Canna," which sounds a lot like canine and "bis" or bi, meaning two – two-dog plant. Sirius is known as the Dog Star in just about every culture, and its brightest star, Sirius A, is known as Canis Major.

All of this leads to the question, why would aliens bring cannabis to us? Either they had good intentions, or nefarious plans. Well, I have it on good authority that the intentions were benefic. In fact, I've been told the Nommos are cosmic nomads who travel around the galaxy, visiting humanoid-occupied planets and planting the herb, like some kind of Johnny Appleseed of cannabis. Hard to believe? Oh, there's more. They are cosmic teachers who will someday return to our planet to see how their cannabis experiment is going here on Earth. If they don't like what they see it could be trouble for the human race.

You see, not everyone in the galaxy thinks like we do here on planet Earth, late in the age of the Kali Yuga. We live in a mentally, spiritually, and environmentally polluted time and space. It has been suggested that the age we live in messes with our thinking. Right now, very few people are able to think Golden Age thoughts, as we are mired in Iron Age, or, Kali Yuga thinking. In a Golden Age there are no need for rules or laws, everyone will live uprightly. Love, for instance, is a Golden Age thought. True love, real love, unselfish, giving love.

Other cultures in other star systems aren't going through the same Kali Yuga age we are and some live with much higher principles than we have. And apparently some extraterrestrial cultures have taken an interest in us along the way, like the Nommos.

Consider these thoughts: What if the Nommos brought cannabis to our planet to alter the course of human evolution? What if this was their way of getting under our skin and changing us from the inside out? What if terrestrial humans are a violent species of mammals that need taming? What if cannabis was introduced to the planet to domesticate humankind?

Or, consider this, what if the Nommos brought us the herb because they knew we'd be going through the Kali Yuga and we would need it?

Man, these Girl Scout Cookies are strong. Just saying.

Fftzoit.

-18-

BIG WINNINGS

Mitch Hopewell only had one true friend in the world, his upstairs neighbor, John Myers. Winning the Lotto for 312 million dollars was going to change that statistic. It was late-2016, and Mitch's life was about to change, big time.

Mitch, like many people, quietly went about his life and did his best to be a good person. He had two cats and kept his apartment clean. Mitch also had a green thumb. Plants just seemed to spring to life around him.

Mitch lived in a four-plex in Long Beach, California, across the street from a liquor store. He had turned the backyard of the apartment building into a beautiful garden. He also had an inside garden with eight beautiful cannabis females growing under 1000 watts of halogen light. This time around Mitch was growing a couple each of White Widow and Northern Lights and four Granddaddy Purple plants. He grew pot for himself and for John upstairs, both of whom had medical recommendations for marijuana.

Mitch worked at an electrical supply company, in the warehouse. He was a talkative and hardworking person. At 57 years old, Mitch was only 5 feet 4 inches tall and fairly muscular.

Mitch also had a wee bit of an anger management problem. Just a bit.

John had gotten to know Mitch when he moved into his building. John was the owner and landlord. He had inherited it and the four-plex next door, from his grandparents. Renting out the other apartments took care of most of his financial needs and John spent a good deal of his time reading and writing. He had been slowly working on "his novel" for over five years. He dreamed of writing the Great American Novel.

Mitch had lived from paycheck to paycheck for years and didn't do a very good job of it. He played the Lotto every week hoping to win at least $10,000 to give himself a financial cushion, something he'd never had.

One Saturday evening he watched the Lotto results on TV: 21, 33, 42, 16, 56 and a bonus number of 3. He looked at his ticket in disbelief. He felt numb. He went on his computer to look up the results and double check the numbers. Sure enough–those were his numbers. Just five minutes earlier Mitch had been trying to figure out how to pay rent that month and now… what would this mean?

Mitch called John upstairs and asked him if he was busy and if he felt like smoking a joint. Mitch had to tell somebody. John said he was just watching something on TV but he'd be down in a moment. When John came down Mitch had a nice fat joint rolled. John came in and sat down on the sofa. Mitch often called John to see if he wanted to get high, so this was an old routine. John loved Mitch's pot. Some people can grow pot and some can't and then some people are really good at growing amazing plants. Mitch was the latter.

Halfway through the joint Mitch asked John what he would do if he won the Lotto?

"Probably what I'm doing now," replied John, "I mean, I like my life and I haven't ever thought of doing anything different. I might give my family some of the winnings. I'd get the plumbing redone in the buildings. Maybe I'd give you a million dollars just so you could pay rent on time. What would you do?"

"I don't know. Quit my job probably. Pay rent on time." Mitch smiled at John.

"I thought you wanted to travel or go live in the Sierras somewhere?"

"Yeah, I just might do that. Buy a motor home and go traveling."

"I could see you doing that. But where would you grow your pot?"

"Maybe I'd get a warehouse, grow a bunch of pot once a year and travel the rest of the time."

"I could see you doing that."

"Guess what?"

"What?"

"I won the Lotto! 312 Million dollars!"

"You're bullshitting, right?"

"No, serious, I won the Lotto tonight."

"Fuckin' A," was all John could say.

"I think I'll pay rent on time from now on," said Mitch, grinning.

-19-

THE NEW SITUATION

Mitch quit his job on Monday and spent the day assessing his new situation. Mitch was going to take this slow, no reason to hurry. John had loaned him several thousand dollars to get him though until the winnings came in. Mitch hadn't felt this relaxed, and anxious, at the same time before. How many nights had he woken up in a panic about finances and getting older? It looked like he wasn't going to be relying on Social Security after all.

Several times during the day he looked at his ticket, to make sure it was safe. He had signed the back of the ticket and was wondering when he'd turn it in. He thought he'd take a road trip and drive to Sacramento to turn it in at the main Lotto office. Maybe John would like to take a road trip too.

He read all kinds of information online about what to do now that he had won all this money. He was going to need lawyers now - lawyers, financial advisers and tax accountants. Taxes were going to take over half of his winnings. Following the advice he read, before he turned in his ticket, he was going to get a new, unlisted phone number.

Mitch made lists of things he needed to do.

Mitch had two daughters from a marriage long ago, both of whom were now married. He would have to set up trusts for them and their families. He waited before he called them and told them the news. Maybe he'd wait until after he turned in his ticket.

Mitch drove up to Sacramento a few days later, by himself. Mitch was nervous about the fact that there would be all kinds of press attention because of his winnings. As it happened the press made a big splash for a minute, and the story of Mitch winning the Lotto was a 30 second news bit. Within 48 hours the press had lost interest in Mitch and his winnings.

Back in Long Beach, one day, while tending to his garden, Mitch thought for a long time that maybe he really would get a warehouse and grow a bunch of pot. John was always telling him how good his cannabis was and it was the thing he liked doing the most.

The tenant renting the other top floor apartment moved out shortly after Mitch won the Lotto and he moved his apartment upstairs next to John's. Downstairs he kept his old apartment and turned it into a large marijuana grow. He turned the kitchen into a room for growing clones, and the living room held over a dozen new plants. He hung a couple 1000 watt halogen lights in the living room.

Marijuana is simple to grow. Marijuana needs air, water and light. About six months after you first plant the seeds you have full grown pot harvested, cured and ready to smoke. Mitch sped up the process by using clones instead of starting with seeds. Clones are cuttings taken from a mother plant. When a clone takes root and starts to grow they're the same genetic age as the mother plant it was taken from, and can usually go to flower as soon as it's grown a few feet tall.

Mitch bought his clones from the collective in Long Beach. He got a bunch of Gorilla Glue #4, Girl Scout Cookies and some OG Kush clones to fill up the living room. He rigged up an exhaust system to carry the smell out the back of the apartment and to flood the plants with fresh air.

After he turned in his ticket it took about eight weeks before the California Lotto started sending Mitch checks. Mitch spent the time looking at RVs. He was thinking about a large van conversion type RV instead of a behemoth-sized road beast. It had to be small enough to feel comfortable on the road, yet big enough for a couple people to live in for months at a time. Mitch was hoping John would hit the road with him.

Mitch's first check for four million dollars arrived two months after he turned in the Lotto ticket. His new financial adviser, George Simpson, suggested he live on a budget of ten thousand dollars a month or less. Mitch thought he might be able to do that. He paid John back the money he had loaned him and then he gave John a gift of $14,000, the maximum he could give without paying extra taxes on the money.

Night after night, when Mitch and John would get stoned, Mitch would try and talk John into going traveling with him. John wasn't much of a traveler. He liked to do his traveling in books, not by car or RV. He had only been on a couple of trips in his life and only one of them had been a good experience. Mitch bought all kinds of travel books and maps and planned a number of possible routes they could take. After a while John warmed up to the travel idea and got into the planning with interest.

First Mitch wanted to drive to New Mexico. Then he wanted to see the Mississippi River. And then New Orleans, or north to Minnesota. He wanted to see the east coast during the fall. He wanted to visit the nation's capital. He wanted to drive and drive and see as much as he could.

-20-
ON THE ROCKS

Dylan's depressions and manias got worse as the rest of the 1990s wore on. Marie was having a hard time dealing with his mood-swings, in spite of the medications he was taking. For weeks at a time he would be in a deep, unreachable, funk. If he wasn't in a funk he was on a manic and creating non-stop. Dylan was also a big flirt when he was on a manic, and spent money like it was water. After a while Marie felt like she was constantly having to deal with Dylan's messes, and she missed the Dylan she used to know. Slowly they were drifting apart.

To make matters worse, Marie was falling in love with her co-worker, a guy named Steve Marshall. Steve worked in another department and they had been having lunches off and on for six months. The attraction was mutual. Marie still loved Dylan though, so she was thoroughly conflicted.

In the late nineties Marie and Steve started having an affair. Dylan and Marie led increasingly separate lives and Dylan had several little flings. It wasn't looking good for Dylan and Marie. They carried on the facade of a marriage for another five years and finally in 2003, a week before the start of the Iraq war, they got a divorce. They had been married nearly twenty years. Their friends went into shock, they thought Dylan and Marie were a great couple.

Marie kept the house in Irvine and Dylan moved to a two-bedroom apartment in Costa Mesa, close to where they had lived years earlier. Dylan was seriously adrift. His studio was gone. His marriage was gone. The life and identity he had built over the last twenty years was gone. Dylan disappeared into a deep depression for months.

There are some people who work in the field of mental health that would say that loss of relationship is one of the leading causes or triggers for a huge episode of depression. I would agree with them. What Dylan went through was like being hit with an atomic bomb.

Marie would come by every so often to make sure Dylan was still among the living. Marie kept saying she wanted to stay friends and she still loved Dylan in spite of everything that had happened. Dylan didn't know what to do with that information at this point.

Dylan needed a studio. An artist without studio space, dedicated studio space, is like a fish out of water. After six months Dylan started to surface from his depression and went looking for studio space in the warehouse area of Costa Mesa. After a short search he found a thousand square foot warehouse that would work perfectly. He got busy setting it up.

The warehouse had a large room in the front where Dylan could hang art, in the back he had room to paint and store his work. The back wall had a huge roll-up door, so Dylan could move large scale pieces in and out of the studio.

Dylan collected all his materials and old paintings from where they were waiting, untouched for months, at Marie's house. It took a weekend, a U-haul truck and help from Marie but everything got moved or thrown away. After the move Dylan and Marie toasted Dylan's new studio with champagne and marijuana and ended up making love on the sofa in the studio. For a long while Dylan would joke that the first thing he made in his new studio was love.

Meanwhile, a spaceship full of stoned Nommos was cruising through the galaxy at several times the speed of light, headed towards Earth. The Nommos had been on their journey for several months, according to Earth time. They were, of course, on Nommo time, which is exactly like Earth time. Why? Because the Nommos originally gave us our time system.

The Nommos were, as I mentioned, very stoned and had been for a long time. They ate, drank and smoked the herb as they traveled the galaxy, planting seeds wherever the opportunity presented itself.

The Nommos were wise beyond belief and knew stuff we couldn't begin to comprehend. They were seriously into hydroponics and a large portion of their ship was a flying hydroponics garden. Being amphibious creatures, they loved to swim through their garden and contemplate the wonders of the galaxy.

Their current mission was a routine visit to Earth to see how the humanoids were coming along after all these years. The Nommos visited every thousand years or so to see how the herb had altered the development of the human species. They had been doing this for 12,000 years, ever since they first brought the herb to the planet. Over the millennia they often would reintroduce the plant to new cultures as needed.

The Nommos believed in love and brotherhood among all species of life. They particularly believed in the sacredness of the herb which they called cannabis, or the two-dog plant. They were, as I mentioned, cosmic nomads dedicated to spreading the love, the herb and their ideas.

Most of our religious ideas have trickled down from things the Nommos had taught different cultures over the many millennia. I wish, from an anthropocentric perspective, I could say that humans came up with our most brilliant ideas, but we didn't. They were handed down to us from various alien species like the Nommos. Also there were the Pleiadians, who visit often, and have brought specific knowledge to individuals. There are also the Orionites, who are the galaxies original gangsters - they bring a lot of bad ideas with them wherever they go. And, of course, there are the various 5th and 6th dimensional creatures that come here for a variety of reasons, not all of them good. Fortunately, there is a police force on the planet to deal with all these alien species, and those are the Men-in-Black.

-21-

ON THE ROAD

Mitch finally convinced John to join him on his first journey in the new RV. Mitch's RV was a van conversion, about 25 feet long and could sleep up to four comfortably. Mitch dubbed his new land cruiser "Lucky", because he said that every ship needed a name. Lucky had hot and cold running water, a flush toilet, a kitchenette, and an awesome stereo system. The outside was in tones of grays, silver and black – very conservative looking. Mitch called it a stealth land ship. He had the name Lucky tastefully painted on the front and back of the RV.

Mitch wanted to wait until after his harvest so they would have some great pot for the road. His plants were already flowering and the buds were starting to thicken. Each plant looked like it would yield at least eight ounces, if not a full pound.

While they waited for the plants to mature they planned the first road trip, a drive up the coast, to Washington and back. They planned on a two week adventure. Mitch said he would do most of the driving if John would navigate and roll joints. This sounded good to John because he'd much rather roll joints and navigate than drive what seemed to him a behemoth vehicle.

They hadn't even started out on the road and a relaxed vibe settled on Mitch and John when they talked about the up-coming trip.

The plants were finally ready to harvest. Mitch cut each plant down and hung them upside down from the ceiling. The idea was to start the drying process. Cannabis plants lose up to 80% of their water content by the time they are finished drying and curing. While the plants hung upside down Mitch went around and cut off all the bigger leaves and kept fans circulating air throughout the room. It took two weeks before the plants were ready to be trimmed.

Trimming is the process of cutting all the buds off of the branches. Then the buds are trimmed further to remove all the little sugar leaves. The sugar leaves are highly potent, so you save those after you have trimmed them. Once the buds are trimmed, they go into mason jars to dry further and cure. The trimming process gets your clippers and your fingers thoroughly sticky with a resinous goo. This sticky substance is rolled off the fingers and the clippers and is used to make finger hash. Finger hash is great to smoke while in the midst of a trimming session. Just saying.

Curing the pot takes another two to four weeks. During that time you open each mason jar and roll it around to circulate the air each day. This lets out accumulated moisture and fills the jar with fresh air. The buds will start to take on their various flavors and lose the vegetative taste as the weeks pass. The cured pot can be stored for months in a cool dark place.

Mitch and John spent several weeks trimming the herb. They had huge sessions where they would trim several ounces at a time. When they were done Mitch had over fifteen pounds. Neither of them had ever seen that much pot in one spot before. Mitch gave John a pound for helping with the trimming.

Mitch had built a special compartment inside Lucky for holding a half pound of pot. He had carefully packaged up several ounces for their first road trip.

It was on April 20th that they started their adventure. They picked that day because it was the stoner's holiday, of course. They called their adventure, *Mitch and John's Big Stoned Adventure,* and were determined to stay high the whole time. Mitch had over forty years of stoned driving experience and felt up to the task.

The first leg of the drive was up highway 101. Well, actually, the first leg of the drive was getting through Los Angeles, but that was nothing but smog and traffic so we'll skip to the 101 somewhere north of the Valley. North of the Valley the hills open up into a rolling terrain of sprawling fields of spring grass, occasional new housing developments and fast food restaurants off the highway. That's when Mitch and John really felt like they were on the road. John took the first pee in the RV while going 65 mph on the 101 near Oxnard. *Now this is traveling,* thought John.

It took eight joints to reach Big Sur from Long Beach. Mitch and John pulled into Limekiln Creek Campground just before the sun set and got a camp site back in the redwoods. It took no time to set up camp and before long they had eaten dinner and had a roaring campfire blazing.

Mitch and John stayed several days in Big Sur. Limekiln Creek had both redwood forests and a beach cove. John was busy writing down notes from their adventure. All this travel was stimulating to the writer in him. Mitch swam in the ocean while John sat on the shore and wrote. Mitch went off on hikes for hours through the forest. John sat and wrote. Together they consumed a number of joints.

"I love being a millionaire," said Mitch, as they sat around the campfire that night.

"I like you being a millionaire too," replied John.

"I don't think I need anything more than this in my life," said Mitch, and he meant it. But that was before he met Darlene.

-22-

DARLENE

Darlene Smith was sitting at the bar in Harvey's Restaurant and Lounge in Washington. She spotted Mitch the minute they walked in the door. Once they were seated she came over and asked if she could join them.

"You are a cute one," she said to Mitch.

Darlene was just a touch over 50 and doing well for her age. She liked to keep herself fit and was still on the look-out for Mr. Right. She was only five feet tall but came on like a hurricane of energy. Mitch, who hadn't been with a woman in several decades, was instantly smitten.

"Where you all from?" asked Darlene.

"Long Beach," answered Mitch, his eyes taking in every inch of Darlene.

"Oh, I lived in Long Beach once," replied Darlene.

"Small world," said John, trying to join in.

"What are you all doing up here in Washington?" asked Darlene.

"Traveling," answered Mitch.

"Oh, I love traveling. I'd hit the road right now if I had someone to go with..." she looked Mitch over as she said this.

The conversation continued for more than two hours. Both Mitch and John had a great time talking with Darlene.

"How about you two park at my place tonight," said Darlene after several glasses of wine.

"Great idea," replied Mitch, with a little too much enthusiasm.

Darlene, who worked as a legal secretary, lived alone in a nice two bedroom cottage on a hill up a bunch of cement steps lined with moss. She gave Mitch and John the grand tour of her cottage.

"Would you like to smoke some great pot?" asked Mitch after they had returned to the living room.

"I'd love too!" replied Darlene. Darlene loved marijuana and smoked regularly.

Mitch got out an ounce of Gorilla Glue #4 from the special compartment in Lucky. He had explained to Darlene earlier how they were on a great stoned adventure and they needed to stay high the whole time, if possible.

"Great idea, I love it!" was Darlene's response. She was so enthusiastic.

The three of them smoked and talked for hours. They talked about all kinds of things, including the Nommos and the Dogon. The only thing they didn't discuss was the Lotto. Mitch kept quiet about that, for now.

-23-
WHAT IF IT'S TRUE?

I can't stop thinking about the Dogon. I need to pause and discuss this for a minute, so, of course this is a good time to light one up.

The Dogon call Sirius B "Po Tolo". They say it's made of a super heavy material not found on Earth. They say that Po Tolo has a fifty year orbit around the Dog Star, which turns out to be true. They also say there is a third star called "Emme Ya," and as we mentioned earlier, this is the star around which the planet of the Nommo orbits. In 1995 two French astronomers announced that they had discovered Sirius C, the star the Dogon called Emme Ya.

Why is this important? Because the herb-loving Dogon said that the Nommos told them about Emma Ya thousands of years ago. I'm starting to feel that the Dogon know what they're talking about. As a matter of fact I'm way beyond just giving them the benefit of the doubt. Especially now that we know a team of Nommos are on their way to Earth.

The Nommos, as it turns out, are just days away from Earth and they are going to be surprised at the changes that have happened since the last team of Nommos visited in the late

900s. The Nommos have a base on the dark side of the moon where they stay during their visits to Earth. From there Earth is just a few hours journey.

The moon, it should be pointed out at this time, is a thoroughly artificial construction. I have that on the word of various authorities in the field. It was constructed by humanoids from Cygnus millions of years ago. They built the moon as a giant space ship to escape the environmental destruction of their planet. They parked it in orbit around Earth millions of years ago. Since then all the old race died off and the moon has become an abandoned ship.

The moon, as a large gravitational object began to alter the evolution of life on the planet as soon as it was placed in orbit. When the gods created humankind several million years ago they took the existence of the moon into account. The cycles of the moon were built into the human system. Every woman is affected by the approximately 28 day cycle of the moon. You could say we were created to evolve that way. At least that's what various authorities say, you can take it with a grain of salt.

Ffftzoit.

-24-

IT'S ALL HAPPENED BEFORE

The Earth, when visited from outer space, resembles a junkyard compound in a vast desert. There is so much space junk: satellites, expended booster rockets, trash from the space stations, and millions of tiny pieces of metal from debris colliding with each other. These pieces of junk are flying around the Earth at thousands of miles per hour. Not only do we have space junk pollution but we have microwaves and cellphone towers everywhere causing strange frequency changes across the globe. Humankind hasn't yet learned to stop polluting their own backyard. The Nommos cried when they arrived.

Last time they visited Earth there were only 300 million people on the planet and now it was bursting at the seams with 7.5 billion humanoids running around. As for cannabis, it was illegal across vast areas and relatively few people were using cannabis as medicine. Humankind had adopted a petroleum-based economy and it was leading to their extinction. Humanity was getting close to doing themselves in again with nuclear war, pollution, violence of all kinds, and runaway technology. The human experiment on planet Earth was going badly, again.

The Nommos had seen humankind do this to themselves

before. Each new age here on Earth also includes the destruction of the civilizations of the previous age. Humans are always beginning again. The previous age had destroyed itself with nuclear war, and the Nommos, who had seen this happen, arrived to help the survivors rebuild civilization.

The Nommos, thousands of years ago, not only brought knowledge to the Dogon but they had also kick-started civilization once again in Mesopotamia, or as we call it today, Iraq. The Nommos' arrival in 3200 BC coincided with the beginning of the Kali Yuga here on the planet Earth.

When the Nommos arrived in 3200 BC they built an underwater palace off the coast of Mesopotamia. At night they would retire to their underwater palace and by day they would come on land and teach the people. They taught people how to grow crops again. They taught people to use cannabis. They taught people to use the teacher plants. They taught people how to build cities. And they gave people knowledge of the stars so humankind would aspire to visit them someday.

The people of Mesopotamia called the Nommos, the Annedoti, which means "repulsive". Apparently the Nommos are not visually appealing to human beings. They were said to resemble ugly bearded men with fish heads and fish tails who, quite frankly, also smelled like fish.

The Nommos traveled around the world finding survivors of the nuclear holocaust. They shared the herb and their knowledge wherever they went. Of course, the standard model of history remembers nothing of the great civilizations that existed during the time history calls the Neolithic Revolution. The truth is huge civilizations existed from 8000 BC to 3300 BC across the globe, and destroyed one another in a great war. All evidence of the ancient civilizations have been buried beneath the sands of time. Off the coast of India are the remains of great cities buried beneath the waves. There are vast areas of that nation that still register the radiation from the great war. The sacred text of the Hindus tell of some of the battles of the great war.

It has been said many times, “This has all happened before and it’ll happen again”.

-25-
PUSH ON THROUGH

Dylan had moved on in life. The severe depressions mellowed out for a while. Marie would come by every so often to visit. They were much better friends now than they had been in years. Dylan started painting again, a good sign of health.

In 2010 Dylan started painting UFOs. He had a rather cartoonish style of painting and his UFOs were both menacing and cute at the same time. The new paintings were a hit with his many collectors and most of the paintings were sold before he had a chance to show them in galleries.

Dylan started to grow his hair out, he was planning on growing dreadlocks. Dylan had always had short, spiky hair, but now he thought he needed a long-term hair solution. Dreadlocks seemed like a good idea.

Dylan was particularly inspired by the Sadhus of India who had massive dreadlocks and smoked vast amounts of pot. Universally dreadlocks are seen as a sign of wisdom and spiritual seeking, and that's where Dylan was when he started to grow his, he was spiritually seeking.

Marie spent a whole weekend turning Dylan's hair into dreadlocks. First she had to separate the hair into small sections, nearly 80 of them. Then each section had to be backcombed, twisted, rubber-banded, and re-backcombed again. This process was repeated over and over until Dylan's head was covered with 80 little dreadlocks.

It was around this time that Marie met a new guy through a friend of a friend, George Simpson, a financial planner, who lived on Balboa Island. George Simpson was a conservative Republican and a deacon at his church, but Marie was still taken with him. They dated for a year before they got married in a small ceremony at a wedding chapel overlooking Newport Harbor.

Dylan wasn't interested in getting another relationship going, but there was a void in his life once Marie was married again. He dated a few times, women he had met at art openings, but no one lit that all important love flame in his heart.

-26-

SADHUS

Many people associate dreadlocks with Rastafarians and Reggae music, which is only part of the picture. Nearly every culture has had people who wear dreadlocks. In many cultures dreadlocks are associated with holy men. Hair is the psychic antenna, and long hair means a better psychic antenna - very important to holy men. Growing dreadlocks seems to come naturally to holy men like Bubba Shiki. So does smoking the herb. Wherever herb is smoked you will find people who take it to holy extremes. And by holy I mean they do it to the exclusion of everything else. Take the Sadhus of India, for example.

The Sadhus have dreadlocks and they smoke huge amounts of pot. They dedicate their lives to Shiva, hit the road and spend their lives stoned. Indian culture makes a place for these strangers in a strange world. These holy men are the only people who can always get away with smoking pot in public. And they smoke lots of pot. It is believed they are removing the sins of the community with their copious amounts of Ganja smoking. A Sadhus' session removes the sins of the hood.

Sadhus. Hair piled high on their heads, naked with ash on their bodies. Holy men and holy mad men. Sadhus by the

Ganges river. Sadhus in the cremation fields. Sadhus covered in death and decay. Sadhus who take away the sins of society.

-27-

MELANIE

Dylan met Melanie Molenski at the little coffee shop by his studio. Melanie worked behind the counter and over the course of several months they had gotten to know each other enough to know they were experiencing a mutual attraction. Melanie went by Mel for short and was about 5 foot 7, with an athletic build. She was ten years younger than Dylan but it wasn't a problem. Mel didn't know anything about art but loved to take photographs.

Melanie had just been through a long term relationship and was cautious about getting into another one so soon. One day Dylan invited her over to his studio, where they got high together for the first time. Mel smoked pot occasionally. Later that evening they watched a couple episodes of *Battlestar Galactica*. Mel had never watched the show because she wasn't into science fiction, but the human side of the story hooked her. She thoroughly enjoyed the whole evening, and her and Dylan started hanging out at least once a week.

For months Dylan and Mel got to know each other as friends before their romance began to blossom. One night, after an art opening, when they were both feeling good from wine and marijuana, they made love at Dylan's apartment. It was early October, the moon was full and the light shone through Dylan's window while they happily fell asleep together.

Dylan and Mel got married a year later, in early October. They rented a little three bedroom house on the east side of Costa Mesa in a residential neighborhood. Dylan was making enough from his paintings, so Mel was able to quit work and the two of them got to hang out together all the time, which is what they enjoyed best, that and smoking the herb.

They also liked to visit Joshua Tree National Park where they would smoke joints around a campfire and watch the skies for UFOs. They discussed how much they loved the hi-desert and started to look for a house. In a few months they found a nice two-bedroom home on a bluff overlooking the Morongo Basin with the view of the National Park that I mentioned earlier in this story. They lived part time in the hi-desert and part time in Costa Mesa for several years before they moved to the hi-desert full time. Dylan rented a storefront in Joshua Tree for studio space. Life was good.

-28-

VIVA LAS VEGAS

Mitch was in love with Darlene. He and John had finished their initial road trip in Lucky the RV and returned to Long Beach. Mitch had started a long distance romance with Darlene. Darlene was also in love with Mitch, even before she found out he had recently won the Lotto. The money was just icing on the cake. She'd had rich men try and date her in the past but money didn't mean a lot to her, it certainly didn't impress her.

John was glad to be back home to his apartment buildings and books. He was kind of glad Mitch had met Darlene because now he wouldn't have Mitch pressuring him about taking another road trip.

They had been back just a few weeks when Mitch took off again for Washington. He and Darlene had planned a little road trip around the northwest. It was to be their *Let's Get Acquainted* road trip. They planned on camping in beautiful and remote locations.

The trip was a big success in every way. Mitch and Darlene got acquainted with each other right away, in the biblical sense of the word. They were as great in the sack together as they were talking on the phone. Everything clicked between them.

They made love everywhere they could across the northwest. And they smoked lots of pot together. Darlene was able to keep up with Mitch, who could out smoke nearly anyone.

Two-thirds of the way through their *Let's Get Acquainted* road trip they decided to head to Las Vegas and get married, by an Elvis impersonator if possible.

Mitch and Darlene got married at the Viva Las Vegas Wedding Chapel. Elvis, in gold lamé, not only officiated the ceremony but he sang four songs to serenade the new couple. It was a beautiful ceremony and captured on video tape for future viewing.

Darlene quit her job now that she was Mrs. Hopewell — a rather wealthy Mrs. Hopewell — and the two of them headed back to Long Beach to get more pot before they went on their Honeymoon road trip.

-29-

FREELANDIA

Alex Von Werner was a multi-billionaire. He was so rich he had stopped counting how much money he had years ago. Now he had a handful of accountants to do that. Alex hated the United States of America, his home country. He considered the U.S.A. to be a failed nation that hadn't collapsed yet. He hated the political class and the entertainment class. He considered people involved in either field to be the lowest of the low.

"Most of them are creeps, sociopaths, pedophiles, or all three," Alex would often say.

Alex wanted to start his own country. He planned to build it offshore, in international waters. He founded a company called Nation Von Werner that did nothing but research his ideas. Alex was a die-hard libertarian. He didn't believe in government restrictions whatsoever. He wanted to build a nation in the middle of the ocean that was a free-wheeling, libertarian mecca. Alex planned to call the country Freelandia.

The first incarnation of Freelandia was an oil rig platform two hundred miles off of the San Francisco coast. The rig was surrounded by a number of large, floating container ships lashed together to create a mile wide floating island. The floating island was off the grid and connected to high-speed internet. Many hi-tech entrepreneurs moved to Freelandia because the rents were cheap, in the beginning.

Von Werner and his team of well-paid lawyers had Freelandia recognized as a sovereign nation by the United Nations. The first industry, besides internet startup companies, that flourished in Freelandia was the marijuana industry. Everyone in Freelandia smoked pot it seemed. A number of huge growing operations were set up in a few of the container ships lashed to the oil rig. The electricity came from a combination of solar, wind and wave action.

The floating city had a desalinization plant to convert salt water into fresh water. It had a number of food growing operations and several grocery chains from the United States had set up operations. They imported tons of soil and created a great park on one of the ships. The currency used on Freelandia was the international alternative currency called Bitcoins. It had hardware stores and electronic stores. They had UPS and FedEx deliveries. The situation was unique, but worked in the beginning.

The first homesteaders on Freelandia were mostly young, idealistic entrepreneurs with a libertarian bent. They moved to Freelandia because they wanted an idea like this to succeed and they were willing to risk everything for an idea. Most of them rarely gave thought to the fact that they were living out a rich man's dream.

Alex Von Werner lived in a huge mansion built on the oil platform. He didn't bother to socialize with any of the other residents of Freelandia. Alex didn't like people. He was, in many ways, a creep and a sociopath himself. These dubious personality traits are what led him to conceive of Freelandia in the first place. He wanted a place where he could do whatever he wanted with no interference. We won't go in depth but to say that Alex Von Werner was mixed up in some seriously nasty shit.

-30-

LIVING THE DREAM

Walter and Nancy Harris lived in San Francisco and dreamed of moving to Freelandia. They watched *Freelandia TV* religiously, which was an internet reality show based on the island nation. *Freelandia TV* was a spoof on reality TV shows and the brain child of Alex Von Werner. The show involved four couples as they went through daily life aboard the floating city while working at an internet start up company that was going big. The show was propaganda for Freelandia, libertarian ideas and the concept of new countries being formed in international waters.

Walter, who didn't smoke pot, would argue politics with anyone who disagreed with his extreme libertarianism. Walter was an idealist of the worst kind, a close-minded idealist. Not that all his ideas were wrong, it's just they weren't right, and certainly not the way Walter argued his points. Nancy, for her part, believed anything Walter told her.

Walter hadn't paid income tax in ten years and the IRS was starting to close in on him. The IRS said he owed nearly a half million dollars in back taxes and penalties. Walter was convinced that if they could get to Freelandia his IRS problems would be over.

There was a lengthy application process to move to Freelandia, not to mention a long waiting list. Fortunately, Walter was a mechanical engineer and Nancy had worked in the health care field as a nurse and both of these areas were in great need in Freelandia. The Harrises were moved up the list and before long they moved to Freelandia.

Walter and Nancy moved aboard the SS Alberta, a decommissioned container ship. Both above and below deck had been converted into really nice lofts and apartments. Walter and Nancy got a lovely, modern two bedroom apartment on the ocean side of the ship, with a view. Walter was immediately employed by Freelandia Waterworks, the company that ran the desalinization plant. Nancy got a job as a nurse at the Freelandia Private Hospital.

There were no income taxes in Freelandia, just a monthly users fee and sales taxes to increase the Freelandia Treasury. Of course, not all the libertarian-minded citizens of Freelandia liked the idea of a users fee, which they called a tax. It really rubbed them the wrong way. These rules had been laid out by Alex Von Werner without any input from the citizens. In his mind it was his country, he could do whatever he wanted. To many other people, it looked like the beginning of a dictatorship.

Freelandia had a government of sorts, with representatives from every ship that made up the island. The Council of Ships, as it was called, had no authority and could only make suggestions and issue declarations. The real power was held exclusively by Alex Von Werner.

Walter joined the first resistance against Von Werner and his budding dictatorship. The sales tax really pissed him off.

"There is nothing libertarian about a sales tax. Not to true libertarians..." he had shouted at Nancy one evening after they had settled in their new apartment. He was wrong about that, but it didn't matter. In Walter's mind taxes made Utopia a little less Utopian. They had never talked about the sales tax on *Freelandia TV* and Walter was feeling let down and misled.

The Resistance needed to get rid of Alex Von Werner and still keep Freelandia alive. It was a nearly impossible idea. Alex Von Werner, for all his faults, was deeply intertwined with Freelandia. It was like trying to remove the head while keeping the body alive.

"The trick," stated Augustus Sey, the leader of the Resistance, at one meeting, "is to grow a new head."

The new head that the Resistance decided upon growing was the Council of Ships. The plan was to get as many Resistance members as possible elected to the council. Once they had a majority of the council seats they would make their move, and challenge Alex Von Werner for control of Freelandia.

Elections for council seats was coming up in three months, plenty of time to put the Resistance's plan into action. On the SS Alberta, Carol Murphy was the Resistance's candidate. Both Walter and Nancy helped out on the campaign by handing out fliers, putting up posters, and making *Carol Murphy for Council* buttons. They talked to every one on their ship about voting for Carol. The campaign was successful and Carol was elected by a wide margin. When the election was over the Resistance had taken 27 out of the 40 seats. Alex Von Werner paid little attention to the election and its results.

The Council began the next term by voting themselves into control of the Freelandia Treasury, for the good of the citizens. After some legal wrangling, the Council's declaration of control over the Freelandia Treasury was declared legal by a United Nations court. The council then used money from the Treasury to buy control of Freelandia Waterworks. The council declared themselves custodians of the water for the people of Freelandia. Revenues from the Waterworks were redirected into the Freelandia Treasury and the power, wealth and influence of the Council of Ships grew.

It took a few years, but by the next election the Council had gained control over large sections of the public life and infrastructure of the floating island. When the next election came around Alex Von Werner wasn't only paying attention but he had his own candidates in the races. Carol Murphy won her reelection, but the Resistance lost five seats on the Council, only holding on to a slight majority. The Resistance continued with their plan to take power away from Alex Von Werner.

-31-

SMOKE BREAK

I've been writing for over a week now and I'm down to half a baggie of pot. I'm hoping to stretch that out until the end of this novel. I'm not rolling my joints as fat as before and mostly resorting to using a pipe instead. A pipe uses less pot than rolling a joint. Especially if you're smoking by yourself.

I just bought a new pipe last week from the smoke shop here in town. They have a basket of ten dollar glass pieces. I keep buying new pipes instead of cleaning them. They last about a month before they get all gunky and either need to be cleaned or replaced. I love smoking from a new pipe.

So, let's catch up to where we are in our story:

Dylan Winslow and Marie Kovak got divorced back in 2003. Since then Marie got remarried to a guy named George Simpson, who is financial adviser to Mitch Hopewell. Dylan also got remarried in 2011, to a young lady named Melanie Molenski.

An ex-con named Louie Gilder briefly entered the story but hasn't been heard from since.

In late 2016 Mitch Hopewell won the Lotto for 312 million dollars and hit the road to Washington with John Myers where he met and fell in love with Darlene Smith. Mitch and Darlene got married in Las Vegas by Elvis, well, an Elvis impersonator.

Meanwhile the Nommos returned to planet Earth and were horrified by what they found. The Dogon, for their part, are doing just what Dogons do in West Africa near ancient Timbuktu, which is tending their cattle, raising crops, smoking the two-dog plant and keeping an eye towards Sirius.

In another part of the world billionaire Alex Von Werner started his own country on a floating island called Freelandia.

As for our real heroine, the lady Mary Jane, my muse, she has been freely and liberally involving herself with the story in so many ways I can't begin to recount. And how does this all tie together? I have no idea yet. These stories are writing themselves. I just sit back, smoke my herb, and observe what's going on. Then I write it down.

Ffftzoit.

-32-
IN THE HI-DESERT

In the hi-desert, close to Joshua Tree, Bubba Ravi Shesha, whose name means Brother Sun King of the Serpents, had established a compound on hundreds of acres of land covered with giant monzogranite boulders. Bubba Ravi Shesha had once been known as Thomas Wilson but that was years ago, in another lifetime.

Bubba was a round fellow. He had a round face and a round body. He was a self-styled spiritual teacher. He believed in reincarnation and believed he was the reincarnation of the original discoverer of cannabis. Bubba also believed in the Nommos. He had seen them before, in his dreams. He had researched the Dogon in depth and had come to the conclusion that the Nommos should be returning anytime now.

Bubba Ravi Shesha had about twenty followers who lived at his compound. Melissa Kingsnake was his right-hand girl and she kept Bubba's small cult together. Everyone in the cult had taken the name of a snake as their last name.

The cult, who were still working on coming up with a formal name for their religion, made most of their money by growing high quality, outdoor-grown marijuana. One of the strains they grew was called Bubba Kush, of course, and was extremely potent. It had a reputation for causing such creativity and euphoria that it should be illegal. It wasn't anymore, not in California where the cult called home. Now, in 2017, marijuana was not only legal to grow but there was a green rush going on and hundreds of investors looked to get into the business.

Bubba's money came from his previous life as an investment broker. One day, back when he was Thomas Wilson, he had finally had enough of the world of finance, walked out and never looked back. That was when he began a long spiritual journey that ended up in the hi-desert, because all spiritual seekers go to the desert at some point. Now the cult had a corporation called Shesha LTD and were legally growing and selling the herb.

Bubba had been given his name by his spiritual teacher Baba Krishna Ravi, and his mantra, Om, Yummie Yummie. After taking a hit of pot, or Ganja, as Bubba preferred to call it, he would say Om, Yummie Yummie.

Bubba Ravi Shesha had dreadlocks which he wore piled up on his head in the style of Shiva, the God of Ganja. He wore long yellow and red robes and sandals. He slept in a tepee in the center of the compound. For years he had dreams about hiking in the mountains and discovering the Ganja plant. The dreams always involved strange fish men who called themselves the Nommos.

The land the cult lived on was called Boulder Gardens by the former owner, and was literally a garden of huge granite boulders. The place had been turned into a desert oasis using permaculture. There were fruit trees and a number of fish ponds. For some reason the area attracted much more rain than the surrounding desert.

Everyone who joined the cult had given all their money and worldly possessions to Bubba Ravi Shesha, in exchange they lived and ate for free in the garden. The cult had its own security force, with Randy Rattlesnake as the its chief. Security, food preparation, drumming, Ganja growing and rolling joints were the most important jobs at the compound.

The compound itself was an acre in size and walled off with a high security fence. Inside the fenced off area were a half dozen buildings surrounding Bubba Ravi Shesha's tepee. The cult had had trouble with outsiders recently, now they took their security seriously.

The cult hosted a drum circle around the fire pit just outside the compound every full moon and new moon, complete with a vegetarian feast. Anyone who wanted to come was invited to join. Bubba Ravi Shesha always had strange and curious tales to tell around the campfire. Bubba was a charismatic speaker and his tales were always the highlight of the evening.

Often Bubba talked about the Nommos, the Dogons, the importance of smoking good Ganja, Sirius, Venusians, Nagas, George Van Tassel, Giant Rock and the Integratron, aliens visiting the desert and ancient Hindu sacred stories. He had a way of weaving many different elements into his tales.

-33-

GIANT ROCK

Here's the history of Giant Rock, as relayed by Bubba around the fire:

"In the Mojave desert, to the northeast of here, is a giant boulder sitting on the desert floor beside a small hill. Some people say this is the largest free standing boulder in the world, but I think that is an exaggeration - I could be wrong. The boulder is called Giant Rock and has a long history.

"For many centuries Giant Rock was a sacred meeting place for the tribes that lived in what is now Southern California, who called it "Giant Stone". The stone was so sacred that only the leaders of the tribes and their shamen could approach it. Everyone else had to stay a mile away. The tribal days came to an end over a hundred years ago and the stone is no longer held sacred by the predominately white culture that now live in the area of the boulder.

"In the early part of the 1900s, a German miner took up residence at the rock. The miner dug under the rock and built himself a home. Once, while picking up mining supplies in Santa Monica, his car broke down and he had it towed to the Van Tassel Garage. Young George Van Tassel, already a pilot, worked with his uncle in the garage repairing cars. The miner, whose name was Frank Critzer, told the pair about his mining operation out in the desert. The Van Tassels agreed to grubstake Critzer with supplies in return for a stake in the mining operation.

"A year later Critzer mailed a map to George and his uncle. George drove out to where Critzer had indicated on the map and was surprised to find a rustic airport with dirt roads leading to it from town. Under the rock he discovered that Critzer had built himself a nice little home. It was a cozy set up that protected the miner from the harsh summer heat and freezing winter temperatures.

"During World War II, Critzer, being German, drew unwanted suspicion because of the shortwave radio antenna he had set up on top of the rock. When the police came out to investigate, Critzer ran into his little home beneath the rock.

"The police asked Critzer to come out but he refused. The police busted down his door and tossed in tear gas to drive him out. The tear gas set off the dynamite Critzer had stored under the rock. Frank Critzer and a police officer both died in the explosion.

"In 1947 George Van Tassel moved his family to Giant Rock to run the airport. George had been working as a test pilot of experimental aircraft and was an experienced flier.

"1947 was a truly significant year. This was the year that flying saucers burst into the consciousness of the world. In July, a UFO crashed near Roswell, New Mexico, which made the front page of newspapers around the world. We were post-World War II and the atomic bomb was on everyone's mind. It was the year microwave ovens were invented, incidentally, and it was the year we moved into the space age and the space race began.

"The Van Tassels leased the land at Giant Rock from the government and operated a small airport there for a number of years. Mrs. Van Tassel, Eva, operated a cafe at the airport called the Come On Inn and had a reputation for making fantastic pies. Howard Hughes was known to fly out to have a piece of Mrs. Van Tassel's pie, often.

"In 1952 George Van Tassel predicted, due to information he had received from aliens, 'the space brothers', that in July spaceships would buzz the White House in Washington DC. George sent letters to the Air Force, *Life Magazine* and the *Los Angeles Herald-Examiner* warning them about the imminent visit. George's predictions came true and twice during July of 1952 the White House was buzzed by strange lights. The Air Force tried to chase the lights but they outran the fastest Air Force jets.

"George believed that the special crystalline structures of the granite boulder were perfect for amplifying the powers of mental telepathy, and began holding channeling sessions under the rock in 1953 to contact the space brothers.

"On a full moon night in August of 1953 the space brothers showed up. The Van Tassels slept outside during the hot summer nights. Around two in the morning George was woken up by a man named Solganda who said, *'I am Solganda, and I would be pleased to show you my craft.'*"

After Bubba did his imitation of Solganda, he paused to take a hit of a joint as it passed by, "Om, Yummie Yummie," he said and then he continued his story.

"As George reported the incident, the man was about 5 foot 7 and would have easily walked down the street without anyone thinking he was odd or different. The man did not say where he was from but he invited George to come on board his ship, which George did.

"The ship was parked a short distance away and George was gently lifted into the ship by an anti-gravity elevator. On board the ship he met three other space brothers like Solganda. The space brothers were deeply concerned about life on planet

Earth because of the atomic bomb. They gave George, who was an engineer by trade, a formula, f=t/1, and said it was the secret to rejuvenating life on planet Earth. It would also allow for time travel.

"George spent the next 25 years of his life turning the formula into a four story, round, wooden building called the Integratron.

"In the fifties and sixties the Van Tassels hosted yearly UFO conventions at the Giant Rock Airport. Thousand of people would come out to the desert to camp, listen to speakers talk about their UFO experiences, and to watch the skies for space brothers who might visit.

"Back in the tribal days it had been prophesied that one day the boulder would split open and a new era would begin. If the boulder split in half then the outlook was not good for the new era, but if the boulder split off just a section then the Earth Mother would bless the new era. Of course, the boulder, which was over seven stories tall and weighed over 100,000 tons hadn't moved in millions of years. The chances of it splitting were slim to none.

"In February of 2000, Judy Freeman and her friends had been camping near Giant Rock. They had come out from Los Angeles to ride off-road vehicles, make out, and party.

"Meanwhile, a shaman had called a prayer gathering of the local shamen because something huge was about to happen. The shaman predicted that Giant Rock was about to split, marking the beginning of a new era. The shaman said they needed to say prayers to the Earth Mother so everything would go well. Throughout the night prayers were said, and sacred herbs were burned.

"Later that morning a ball of lightning shot from north to south through the house where the shamen had gathered. In a couple of minutes another ball of lightning shot through the house from east to west. Four shamen and prayer warriors watched this happen. The shaman who had called the others together declared that the lightning was a sign that the Earth Mother had accepted their prayers.

"As Judy later reported the events on an internet forum, she found herself awake around four in the morning. As she watched, the boulder, inexplicably, began to rock back and forth for a few minutes, when suddenly, a third of the boulder split off and fell to the ground."

Bubba stopped talking and let his story sink in. He sat down and the drumming began.

-34-

GIANT ROCK, POSTSCRIPT

I've visited Giant Rock and I was disheartened. This was back in 2009. We drove out there with a few friends. I had never been to a desecrated sacred site before. The spirit around the boulder was dense and heavy with a negative vibe. The boulder was covered with graffiti and the air was filled with the sound of off-road bikes and ATVs. We stayed for five to ten minutes before we had to leave, it was too heavy. Not what I had been expecting at all. I'm amazed the Earth Mother accepted the prayers of the shamen because the site has been defiled beyond belief. It was so sad.

Eyot.

-35-

TIMELESS ONES

Time, as we mark it off, with 60 seconds making a minute, 60 minutes making an hour, and twenty-four hour making up a day, is something that was handed down to us from the Sumerian people. The Sumerians, of course, learned it from the Nommos. The Nommos wore waterproof wrist watches and considered time to be of utmost importance.

In Freelandia there were a small group of people who had stopped wearing watches and tried their best to ignore time. They recognized that the world worked according to time but they did what they could to stamp out the footprint of time, wherever possible. They called themselves the Timeless Ones. They ate when they were hungry and slept when they were tired. They said they lived in the great now. Because they operated outside of time, the Timeless Ones never procrastinated, they just did things immediately or waited until the moment was right to work on a project. Events unfolded in a natural and organic way.

"A watch is a ball and chain," said Augustus, who had quit the Resistance and had joined the Timeless Ones.

Freelandia, in general, wasn't thrilled by the Timeless Ones, but put up with them in their anarchist and libertarian way.

Bubba Ravi Shesha, who read about the Timeless Ones online, thought they were on to something and spent some time trying to figure out how to work their ideas into his cult. Of course, it was going to require some modifications, they were, after all, marijuana farmers and time was useful to them. Plants had to be watered at certain times, the plants flowered after a certain amount of time, drying and curing the buds took a certain amount of time.

Bubba called his modification *Simple Time*. Second and minutes were to be ignored, hours could be noticed, but it wasn't encouraged.

"Time," said Bubba, "should pass unnoticed. Do things in the moment of need. Don't let a clock rule your life."

The cult, who thought the Timeless Ones had come up with a great name, set about trying to come up with an appropriate and descriptive name of their own.

"I think the name should say something about who we are," offered Randy Rattlesnake at one cult meeting, stating the obvious.

"I think we should be the Sheshaites," suggested Sandy Cornsnake, but the way she said it, the words came out sounding like "She shits" and her idea was voted down by the rest of the cult.

"How about something exotic, like The Snake People," suggested Melissa Kingsnake "or the Serpent People?"

"How about the Shivanistas, or the Naganites?" threw in someone sitting near the back.

"Naganites... I like that," said Melissa. There was a murmur of appreciation among the assembled cult members.

The Nagas are an ancient race of serpents who participated in the creation of the world. They turned consciousness into the material world by churning the milky sea of creation with their great bodies. Bubba often taught about the Nagas. The Nagas were why the cult members had all taken snake names.

Several other names were thrown around but after the evening was through Naganites was voted in as the new name.

-36-

GROWING PAINS

After a few years Freelandia began to grow. Alex Von Werner had bought a French engineering firm called SeaLegs that specialized in designing unique living situations on water. Freelandia became SeaLegs' only project. The firm designed a floating harbor around Freelandia and envisioned the offshoot of various other floating islands connected to Freelandia.

A number of new container ships were added to the island mass, and before the harbor was built Freelandia had grown to five square miles. The Council of Ships had increased to 120 seats and was beginning to discuss the idea of establishing a Constitution. The influence of Alex Von Werner had decreased, while the Council's influence had increased.

Alex was getting used to the idea he wasn't going to be running the show. He had other activities to keep himself busy with, like his new plan to launch a city in space. He sold off his remaining interest in Freelandia to the Council of Ships, maintaining his mansion on the oil rig.

Von Werner was darn proud of himself. He had pulled off the biggest project he could possibly imagine, up until now. The more Alex thought about a space city, and he thought about it a lot, the more excited he became. He wanted to call the city Spacelandia.

The Resistance was no longer *the Resistance,* they had become the status quo. They called their political party the Freelandia Party and many of them were becoming unbearable politicians. Such is the way of things. Politics always ends up attracting politicians.

Soon, a new opposition party formed called Freedom For Freelandia, or the Three Fs Party, which was not a good name at all. The Three Fs wanted to abolish the users fee that the Resistance had never eliminated. They also wanted to abolish the sales tax and shrink the size of the ever-going new government.

The government decided, in an unpopular move, to declare large portions of the oil rig platform as government territory. All the available space around Alex Von Werner's mansion was appropriated by the government and new construction began.

Walter Harris joined the Three Fs Party. He told Nancy he liked the cut of their jib.

"I like government to be small enough you can drown it in a bathtub," remarked Walter often, repeating something he heard somewhere in the past. Walter wasn't in favor of all the government's new building plans.

This isn't going to turn out good for the people, he thought to himself. *Maybe something needed to be done to make a statement.*

Walter thought about bombs for the next two weeks. The idea of bombing the new construction, to make a statement, became a solid reality in his mind and he got to work making some plans of his own.

-37-

NAGANITES

On the first full moon after the Spring Equinox the cult initiated their new name. From now on they would be known as Naganites. Also, the name Boulder Gardens was abandoned and a new name was established, Nagaland. Not to be confused with the mountainous state in northeast India.

The Naganites believed in the divinity of the ancient Nagas and played drums as a sign of worship, of veneration. They also believed in reincarnation.

"You're coming back again, so treat the planet nice," was Bubba Ravi Shesha's advice. Sound advice for anyone, I'd say.

The ancient Nagas were semi-divine serpent men and woman who were incredibly beautiful. They had human torsos and heads with a canopy of seven cobras rising up from behind their shoulders. They had the lower body of a serpent. Their deep underground kingdom is called Naga-loka and is full of beautiful palaces, rich in culture, music and the arts, not to mention precious gems and metals.

Those who are in the know are aware that the Nagas are the ones behind the scenes that pull the strings of those who pull the strings in the world. Unbeknownst to Bubba and the Naganites, the Nagas didn't have our best interests in mind.

The Nagas were planning on taking over the planet some day soon, and were well on their way to accomplishing their goal. Long ago the Nagas used to live on the surface of the planet, but their numbers increased to the point where they covered the Earth. Vishnu, who was the preeminent God of the time, launched a war against the Nagas to drive them underground. He would ride into battle against the Nagas on the back of his immortal friend Garuda. Garuda is a giant man-like creature made of gold who has an eagle's head and giant wings. Now that both Vishnu and Garuda weren't around any more, the Nagas saw an opportunity to return to the surface.

Also unbeknownst to the Naganites was that acres back in boulders, in an unexplored area, was an entrance deep into the Earth. The entrance led all the way to one of the Nagas' great underground cities.

-38-

GUY FAWKES DAY

Walter kept his plans to himself, he didn't even tell Nancy. No reason to involve anyone else. This was going to be a one-man operation. He had chosen November 5th for the date of the bombing because that was Guy Fawkes Day. Getting the necessary explosives for the job was a piece of cake. Not too surprisingly, weapons and explosives were readily available on Freelandia.

Over a few months Walter was able to acquire a large stash of C-4 plastic explosives. Being a member of the Freelandia Waterworks engineering team he had no problem accessing the new construction that was happening on the oil rig platform.

Every few days he carefully concealed several packages of C-4 on the oil rig, with timers set for 6:00AM on Guy Fawkes Day. No one was expecting such an attack and no one ever found any of his concealed packages. By the time the special day had arrived hundreds of packages of C-4 had been placed all over the platform. You could say that Walter had been a little over zealous with his plans.

At 6:00 on Guy Fawkes Day explosions began to rip through the oil rig platform. Alex Von Werner's mansion was only one of the unintended victims of Walter's plan. The oil rig platform wasn't built to stand that many explosions pulling the rig in so many directions at once. The legs of the platform buckled and crumpled and it collapsed into the ocean.

The explosions rocked all five square miles of Freelandia. The huge flotilla of container ships broke apart and busted through the walls of the harbor. Many ships close to where the oil rig platform had been were pulled underwater with the collapsing platform. Because the ships had all been decommissioned they had no engines, so about 100 container ships, now full of refugees, went adrift in the Pacific Ocean. Several ships ran into each other and sank.

The SS Alberta survived the initial explosions and drifted out to sea. Walter and Nancy's apartment was wrecked and the ship was slowly taking on water. Nancy, unfortunately, got thrown violently by the effects of the first explosions and smashed her head against a steel wall and wasn't breathing anymore. After three days the SS Alberta sank. Walter and a few other survivors built a flotilla of trash and anything else that would float, and left the ship before it slipped under the waves. They floated around for several harrowing weeks but eventually floated into San Francisco Bay and were saved. Walter vowed never to go out on the water again.

Walter's Guy Fawkes Day plan had completely destroyed Freelandia. Alex Von Werner was never found. Augustus survived. He was rescued a few days after the explosions. Carol Murphy, who had grown to be quite a formidable politician in Freelandia's Council of Ships, survived and vowed to re-build Freelandia. Alex Von Werner's will had made sure that billions of dollars went to the Nation Von Werner corporation to insure that more sea island nations could arise in the future.

-39-

AUGUSTUS

After insurance from the destruction of Freelandia had taken care of Augustus Sey, he had a nice half million dollars in the bank. He traveled south from San Francisco and ended up in Joshua Tree. Augustus didn't know what he wanted to do with his life now. He had just turned thirty and was still idealistic. He didn't know if he wanted to be a part of Freelandia 2. It had been a fun adventure but now he was looking for something else.

On a bulletin board outside a coffee shop he saw a flier for the upcoming full moon drum circle at Nagaland, which was that night. The flier peaked his interest. He had heard the word Naga somewhere before but he couldn't remember where.

From Joshua Tree it took just over a half-hour to drive out to Nagaland. It was back in an area called Pipes Canyon, up a long dirt road. Augustus had rented a Jeep for his travels and had all his camping gear with him. He also had about an ounce of prime OG Kush buds, because you always have to be prepared.

When Augustus arrived he was greeted by Melissa Kingsnake. She showed him where he could set up a tent and told him the feast would begin in an hour. Augustus set up his tent and found himself thinking about Melissa, a lot.

The Naganites were all vegetarians, except Bubba Ravi Shesha, who liked to have a hamburger every so often. Sandy Cornsnake was in charge of the kitchen, and she was a strict vegetarian along with being a fantastic cook. The vegetarian feast was truly a feast, and all of it grown organically in Nagaland. Augustus, who had been a vegetarian for years, was seriously impressed. Not only that, but Sandy was kind of cute and caught Augustus' eye, pushing thoughts about Melissa out of his head.

Throughout the feast joints of Bubba Kush were passed around, creating not only a feast for the senses but for the mind. Augustus was feeling at home among the Naganites. The drum circle was especially good this evening. Danny Greensnake had composed chants to honor the Nagas and several people played didgeridoos which created deeply mystical sounds as their tones intertwined.

The pounding of the drums, the chanting and the didgeridoos blended together and spread out over Nagaland. The pounding sounds reverberated off of the boulders. The sounds penetrated the entrance to the deep underground. The pounding traveled to the sensitive ears of some Nagas deep, deep underground. They listened with intense interest to the words being chanted and started to head towards the surface. The Nagas are a curious species.

Augustus camped out with the Naganites for several weeks and became increasingly interested in the cult as the days went by. He helped in the kitchen for the next vegetarian feast and drum circle. He also joined the joint rolling team.

What really inspired Augustus, besides Sandy Cornsnake, was the stories Bubba Ravi Shesha told at the drum circles and at breakfast everyday. After several weeks among the Naganites, Augustus presented Bubba Ravi Shesha a cashiers check for several hundred thousand dollars and said he wanted to become a Naganite.

A two-day celebration of feasting, drumming, chanting, and Ganja smoking was planned to welcome Augustus into the Naganites. Melissa and Sandy worked together to dread Augustus' long hair for the event. On the first night of the celebration Bubba gave him his new name, Augustus Cobra. Later that evening he kissed Sandy for the first time.

-40-

NAGAS FOR REAL

"Let me tell you about my namesake, Shesha," started Bubba Ravi Shesha as the drums mellowed down to a low murmur on the second night of the celebration.

"Shesha was a Naga, a great Naga prince. He was very spiritual. He practiced an aesthetic form of penance before the Gods."

Bubba paused to light up a massive joint and take in a deep hit.

"Om, Yummie Yummie," he said as he passed the joint to Melissa on his left hand side.

"The form of penance Shesha performed involved extreme fasting and difficult yoga positions. Brahma, one of the preeminent Gods, noticed Shesha and was impressed. He approached Shesha and asked him to hold the world in his dreaded hair. Shesha agreed and went down a hole in the ground to the bottom of the Earth and hoisted the world into his dreads."

Bubba paused as another joint came around and he took a big hit, "Om, Yummie Yummie". Then he continued his story. He talked about Shesha for a bit more and then veered into talking about the Nommos and the start of civilization. He talked about frequencies and the way cellphones effect us, and segued into talking about sound and the Integratron. He ended his tale by talking about the importance of drumming for your spiritual well-being.

The drumming began again in earnest and the joints continued to pass around. Drumming, feasting and smoking continued for several hours as the Naganites celebrated.

Later that night, Sandy and Augustus slept together in Augustus' new room. The compound got quiet and still around three in the morning.

That's when the Nagas showed up. They had been drawn by the drumming, the chanting and the copious amounts of Ganja smoke. Being naturally curious creatures they couldn't help themselves.

That night Kevin Diamondback was on security duty with Randy Rattlesnake. He nearly pissed his pants when he saw the three Nagas, each about fifteen feet long, slither up to the compound. He heard them as they spoke in their native tongue, which, of course, sounded like snakes talking.

The Nagas explored around the fire pit and circled the growing garden before heading back to the boulders, to the opening that led back home underground.

Kevin, who was shaking when he finally found Randy, had been able to take several good photos of the Nagas with his phone. When they played back the security camera footage they were amazed to watch the three well-dressed Nagas slithering around the outside of the compound.

Bubba was amazed when he watched the footage after breakfast that morning. Nagas really existed! He had been spinning tales of Nagas for so long he had started to believe they were just tales, not bits of truth cloaked in stories.

-41-

SOUL SEARCHING

Most of the Naganites were beside themselves with the reality that Nagas, actual, real Nagas, had visited their camp. And they had photographic evidence to prove it. It wasn't spoken about out-loud, but more than a few Naganites thought that Augustus was somehow responsible for the arrival of the Nagas. Never had anything like this happened before Augustus showed up. There was a mixture of admiration and distrust.

Augustus, for his part, was both amazed and a bit confused, he was wondering what he had stumbled into here. Nagas. Real live humanoid serpents, about fifteen feet long, had visited the camp. This was some crazy shit.

Sandy, for her part, was overjoyed at the arrival of the Nagas. "Isn't this what we're about," she kept saying. She felt her life's mission was coming to fulfillment.

Bubba started doing some serious soul-searching once the initial excitement died down. He really didn't believe in his heart most of the stuff he talked about. I mean, when it came down to it. It was just a routine he had developed over the years that he was really good at performing. He had that gift of spinning a yarn. There had been a time when he really thought he was the reincarnation of the original discoverer of Ganja, but that had faded as a present reality. Now he was just a guy going through the motions. And he liked the sweet young people his stories attracted. It had been fun with the snake names and all, but now this was some serious business.

Now he had photos and video tape of actual Nagas, or serpent people, or whatever they were, and he no idea what to do. Here were all these innocent kids, hanging onto his every word, and he had no idea what to say.

Melissa Kingsnake rose to the occasion and led the Naganites while Bubba went on a private spiritual retreat. She kept all the regular business going; after all, there were plants to water and maintain, meals to cook, clothes to wash and all the routine activities of running the cult. Bubba Ravi Shesha borrowed the house of a musician friend he knew in Joshua Tree to get away from Nagaland for a while.

-42-
THE FIRE DREAMER

Louie Gilder wanted to go out to the desert for his birthday. He didn't have anyone to go with, so he planned his own trip to Joshua Tree for the following month. Louie wasn't going to look for UFOs or aliens, he just needed some time out in the open. He had seen an article in the *Los Angeles Times* about Joshua Tree and it seemed like the kind of open space he needed.

Louie drove a Dodge minivan which was weathered from age. The van was originally teal but now the paint had oxidized into abstract patterns. Louie did the best he could to keep his van nice but it was an uphill battle. For the trip Louie bought himself a new tent, sleeping bag, camp stove, ice cooler and a camp chair in a big shopping splurge that set his savings back.

When the time for Louie's vacation arrived he was on the road by five in the morning, headed straight to Joshua Tree National Park. At 8:30 he was having coffee at Natural Sister's coffee shop in downtown Joshua Tree. Louie had driven out on a Tuesday and found himself a camping site in the Hidden Valley Campground, one of the best campgrounds in the park, in my opinion.

Hidden Valley is a place where cattle rustlers used to hide out over a century ago. It has numerous, huge monzogranite boulders, and is now a world famous rock-climbing destination. Louie got a campsite off of the main loop, a little back from the road. He set up camp and settled down with a good book to read.

It was hard to read because he kept getting distracted by the rock climbers and the surrounding beauty. He wished he had someone to talk to about the things he saw. The day was particularly clear and the light reflecting off the boulders had a lustrous quality.

Some time around dusk a girl came wandering into his camp while Louie was making a dinner of chili, hot dogs and corn bread.

"Mm, that smells good," said the girl.

"Excuse me," said Louie.

"Your dinner smells good. I was just commenting on that," replied the girl.

"Can I help you?" asked Louie.

"Do you want to see a fire dance? I do fire dances," said the girl.

"A fire dance would be... different, interesting..." Louie stammered. He had never seen a fire dance, and had no idea what this girl was talking about,"What's a fire dance?"

"I'll show you, but it'll cost twenty-five dollars. I have to pay for fuel, you know."

"What's your name?"

"Karina the Fire Dreamer," replied the girl.

"Karina the Fire Dreamer? That's the name your parents gave you?" asked Louie.

"You can call me Karina, my parents did and they're about as old as you are."

"You can call me Louie, just like my parents did."

"Nice to meet you, Louie. You want a fire dance or what?"

"Is this legal?"

"If the ranger comes around, just say I'm camping with you, okay?"

"Okay, I've got twenty-five dollars, I guess this will be the only time I'll ever see a fire dance, so why not."

"Cool, can I have a bite of your dinner too?"

"Sure, there's enough for two."

"Awesome, let me go get my stuff." Karina disappeared for a few minutes and came back with a backpack, a sleeping bag and a large shopping bag.

The two of them ate dinner and got to know each other a little. Karina was a camp gypsy of sorts. She made her living, if you could call it that, doing fire dances and sleeping wherever someone was kind enough to let her join their campsite. The rangers weren't too fond of Karina and she did her best to stay out of their way.

Louie lit a fire after dinner and soon it was blazing.

"You ready for my fire dance?" asked Karina.

"Absolutely," answered Louie.

"Okay, first I have to change. This will take a couple minutes." Karina grabbed her bag and disappeared behind some bushes. After a couple of minutes she reemerged wearing a bikini top and a flowing skirt wrapped around her waist. From each of her hands hung a little pot of fire on a long chain. Slowly, and with serpentine motions, Karina began to move around the campfire, swinging the pots of fire. Soon Karina was making beautiful patterns in the air, while dancing around in circles. Louie was entranced. He had never seen anything like it in his life. For fifteen minutes Karina moved around with the fire and then slowly the dance came to an end.

-43-

EDUCATING LOUIE

Karina camped out with Louie for the next few days. He paid for several more fire dances, but mainly because he thought Karina was interesting and he wanted to spend more time with her.

Karina had grown up on a commune in Oregon and liked the gypsy lifestyle. She had been on the road for several years. She had recently turned twenty-one and was slowly saving up money to return home to visit the commune.

Louie told her about how he got busted years ago and how going to prison had changed him. Now he was clean and sober, living the straight life.

“Really, you don’t smoke the herb?” asked Karina, the second evening they were hanging out.

“Nope. I haven’t in over fifteen years. Don’t plan too. I hear the stuff they have today is way stronger than back then.”

“Sure it’s stronger but it takes less to get you high.”

“Do you smoke weed?” asked Louie.

“Oh yes, but I prefer to call it the herb. I have some stuff right now that is so delicious and has such a mellow high, do you mind if I have a smoke?” asked Karina.

"No, go right ahead. I haven't even smelled weed... the herb, in ages. I used to like the smell of the herb."

Karina got a cigar box out of her backpack. She rolled up a joint. After a minute she lit it, took a big hit, and held it in. She blew the hit out in Louie's direction and then coughed several times. After she took another hit Louie motioned for her to hand over the joint. Louie took a little hit, and then a bigger hit and passed the joint back.

"Man, that tastes good," said Louie as he accepted the joint back from Karina. He took another big hit, and could start to feel the herb spreading through his body.

"Now, I'll do my fire dance," said Karina after they finished the joint.

"Awesome," was all Louie could say.

The fire dance was way beyond the previous night's version. Karina seemed to move smoother and with greater skill, spinning the fire pots in more intricate patterns. Louie clapped along in time with her dance. The dance seemed like it lasted for hours, but only lasted about fifteen minutes.

"Where did you learn to do that?" asked Louie after Karina sat back down.

"I hung out in Long Beach for a while, and learned it from a girl named Serena," replied Karina.

"I live in Long Beach," said Louie.

"Small world," said Karina, smiling.

"Yes it is, and it seems to be getting smaller all the time."

"Huh, what do you mean by that?"

"I don't know."

The conversation drifted for a bit until Karina brought up UFOs, aliens and the Nagas. It seems like most conversations in the hi-desert turn to UFOs at some point. Louie had never been interested in UFO discussions until Karina talked about it. Now it seemed deeply interesting. Karina talked for a while about several UFOs she had seen, about dancing at the Integratron, about Nagaland and the groovy Naganite drum circles, and about the mysterious Nagas of old. Karina had picked up a lot of information along the way.

"You seem wise beyond your years," said Louie after a while, "I mean, you know about a lot of stuff I've never heard of before."

Karina paused while she was rolling up a fresh joint. She nodded in agreement. She was starting to like this Louie Gilder person.

You might think that Karina was a loose kind of girl because of her gypsy ways, but you'd be wrong. Karina had only slept with one person in her whole life, and that was years ago. She was a very particular girl who knew how to take care of herself. Just saying.

-44-
LOUIE IN NAGALAND

Louie camped out for several days and, sadly, knew he had to get back to Long Beach and work. He had really been enjoying Karina's company. After a few days it seemed like they were existing in their own little world but Louie couldn't stay forever, no matter how he felt.

"I have to go back to Long Beach," said Louie, remorsefully, on his last morning of camping.

"I've been really enjoying hanging out with you," said Karina, genuinely sad that Louie was leaving.

"What are you going to do now?" asked Louie.

"More fire dancing, unless you want to give me a ride somewhere," answered Karina.

"Where do you want to go?"

"Nagaland."

"Is it far from here?"

"Not really."

"Sure, I'll take you there."

"Cool, the Naganites are really groovy and they'll let me camp out for a while. They love the fire dancing."

Louie packed up his camp and by mid-morning they were

ready to leave. Nagaland was about forty-five minutes away and before lunch they were pulling up at the gate. Melissa Kingsnake saw them as they pulled up and was delighted when she saw Karina get out of Louie's minivan.

"Fire Dreamer!" yelled Melissa as she ran out to greet them.

"Kingsnake!" called back Karina.

After they had exchanged hugs, Melissa motioned everyone over towards the compound.

"What are you doing here? We've missed you so much," said Melissa to Karina.

"I've been in Jtree, earning some money doing fire dances," replied Karina, "do you think Bubba would mind if I say here for a few?"

"Bubba wouldn't mind at all. Everyone will be glad you're back. Do you think you'll stay for the next drum circle?"

"That was my plan. I need to meditate and hear the words of Bubba again."

"Well, you're welcome to stay as long as you like. Sandy sure would love to have you help out in the kitchen again."

"That's what I was hoping," replied Karina, who was definitely feeling the need for some of Sandy's vegetarian food.

Louie spent the rest of the day with Karina and the Naganites. He got the grand tour from Melissa and was amazed at the Ganja growing operation. It had been years since he had seen a marijuana grow, but he felt at home as he walked among the plants.

"These are some beautiful ladies," said Louie after spending a little time in the garden.

Melissa introduced Louie to Tony Mamba, the Naganite in charge of the growing team. They hit it off right away. Louie told Tony he was a gardener and about how he got busted years ago for growing marijuana. Tony shared a bit of his history and how he came to live at Nagaland. They smoked a bowl of Bubba Kush together. The day turned into a delightfully stony afternoon and Louie never wanted to leave.

-45-

LUNG ISSUES

Sometime in late 2017 Dylan developed a bad cough that worried Mel. The cough got so bad that whenever he moved he would break out into a spasm of coughing that brought up some serious gunk from his lungs.

Dylan hadn't taken good care of his lungs over the years. Back when he was a mod he smoked unfiltered clove cigarettes, which probably aged his lungs about ten years in the few years he smoked them. Then Dylan smoked cigarettes, Marlboro Light 100s, for a dozen years. He would still be smoking cigarettes if the voice of God hadn't spoken to him one January morning back in 1997. The voice of God had said, "Dylan, you're killing yourself," as he was lighting up a cigarette from a fresh pack. Dylan put out his cigarette immediately and never smoked again. You don't fuck with the voice of God.

The cough continued for a couple of days and both he and Mel realized that it wasn't going away, they'd better have it looked at by a doctor. On Friday they drove to an urgent care facility in Yucca Valley. The doctor took one look at Dylan's X-rays and told Dylan and Mel that they had a choice, get to an ER immediately or go home and Dylan would probably die.

Not much of a choice.

Dylan and Mel drove to the Hi-Desert Medical Center Emergency Room immediately and got in to see a doctor right away because the urgent care facility had called ahead.

"My biggest fear," Dylan told Mel as they waited, "is that they'll stick an IV in me, and I'll have to stay overnight and not be able to go home."

Shortly after this a nurse showed up to put an IV in Dylan's arm and they wheeled Dylan off to have a CAT-scan. Dylan's worst fears were starting to materialize.

After five hours in the emergency room, the doctor came up to Dylan and Mel and told them that Dylan had an abscess the size of a fist in his lung. It was in the lower part of the left side. What Dylan was coughing up was the infection from the abscess, which was starting to break up. If the abscess broke up completely it would get into Dylan's bloodstream and poison his whole body. The doctor wanted to admit Dylan to the hospital immediately.

Dylan spent the next eleven days in the intensive care unit as doctors worked hard to remove the abscess without resorting to surgery. They had to insert a tube through his back into his lungs to pump high-powered antibiotics directly into the abscess and to drain the wound. Dylan was, thankfully, oblivious to how sick he was. No one really told him until he got out of the hospital, it was only then that he came to understand how seriously close to death he had come.

Dylan, Mel and the doctors tried to figure out how Dylan had gotten this abscess but they couldn't find any answers. Dylan was straight forward about his pot smoking, but surprisingly, none of the doctors considered that to be a factor.

Dylan was shaky and unsteady when he got out of the hospital. He had lost about twenty pounds, most of it muscle, the nursing staff informed him. A team of nurses had installed a long-term IV into his upper arm called a PICC line, so Mel could give him IV antibiotics every day for the next month.

Even though the doctors had assured Dylan that cannabis had nothing to do with his abscess, Dylan was leery about smoking again. The hospital experience had really shaken him up. It caused him to reevaluate everything in his life, especially marijuana smoking.

"Just my luck," Dylan joked to Mel one morning while she was setting up his IV, "marijuana becomes legal, and I have to quit smoking."

"We'll see," replied Mel, who knew Dylan well.

-46-

BUMP IN THE ROAD

"It's a big country, and there are a lot of places you can live," Mitch said to Darlene one afternoon as their RV, Lucky, sailed smoothly across the asphalt of a superhighway in a southwest state. They were currently on their way back to Long Beach after a month-long Honeymoon.

"But I haven't seen anything that makes me want to stay more than a few days," replied Darlene. Darlene was busy rolling an afternoon joint. She had become experienced at joint rolling over the last few months.

"Rest area ahead. Let's pull in and have some lunch and a smoke," said Mitch.

"I liked Colorado and they have legal pot. But I don't know where I'd want to live in Colorado," offered Darlene.

"I liked Colorado too. Hmm, that's a good option," replied Mitch as they pulled into the rest area.

Mitch and Darlene had been looking wherever they traveled for a place they might want to live in a more permanent fashion. Colorado was looking good to the newlyweds, as were the Earthships near Taos, New Mexico. They had stayed for several days in an Earthship and had been impressed by the design.

An Earthship is a round structure that uses recycled tires and adobe as its main building material. They are completely off-the-grid, and collect rain water for drinking and washing, and solar rays for electricity. Mitch and Darlene were looking for something a little different. Being new millionaires gave them lots of options. They wanted somewhere with land. Somewhere they could have a few acres to themselves eventually, but they were in no hurry.

They had been enjoying this life on the road. The world is a different place when you're on the road, you see everything differently. They loved waking up in different places nearly everyday. Sometimes they would linger at a particular campsite for a few days, if the site was scenic and private, but mostly they liked being on the move.

After weeks of travel Mitch had his first road rage incident in months. It started with a small thing, when he was cut off by a beige Toyota driven by a little old lady who didn't even realize she had pulled in front of the RV. Mitch hadn't been sleeping well for several days and was feeling more than a bit frazzled.

First Mitch pulled the RV up close to the Toyota until he was tailgating the poor old lady. This freaked Darlene out, who hadn't seen this side of Mitch yet. Next Mitch jerked the RV to the left and floored the gas until he had passed the Toyota and jerked the RV back into the right lane and hit the breaks, nearly causing the Toyota to rear end Lucky. Meanwhile Darlene was yelling at Mitch as Mitch was yelling at the Toyota. Then Mitch hit the gas and hauled it out of the little town they were passing through.

"What the fuck was that?" yelled Darlene as they started to slow down a few minutes later.

"Stupid bitch in that Toyota cut me off on purpose!" Mitch yelled back.

"First off, never call a woman a bitch in my presence, OK.

Second of all, she was an old lady. I don't think she even saw you."

"It was on purpose."

"No, Mitch, it wasn't on purpose."

The arguing went on for several minutes, then a tense silence settled over the RV.

-47-
BUBBA'S FUNK

What is a spiritual leader to do when they realize they've lost their way and are confused about their faith? Bubba Ravi Shesha was in a deep funk. His friend had loaned him one of his rental units in Joshua Tree for a personal retreat. He knew he couldn't stay away from Nagaland for long.

For the first few days of his retreat Bubba didn't get out of bed, except to go to the bathroom. He was on a fast, from food and herb, looking for spiritual insight.

Bubba knew all kinds of history about the Nagas but all his knowledge hadn't prepared him to deal with real live Nagas. If Nagas were real what else that he'd been talking about was real, Bubba wondered? What about the Nommos? What about the two-dog plant, was that really an alien plant? And what about George Van Tassel and the space brothers? Were there space brothers that could be contacted? They had somehow contacted the Nagas, and… Bubba's mind spun in circles.

It took another week but Bubba was soon able to wrap his mind around these new realities. He didn't have to change his beliefs, he just had to take them to heart and actually believe in his beliefs, which can be harder than one thinks.

And what did Bubba Ravi Shesha say he believed, you might ask?

Bubba believed in reincarnation. He believed he was the reincarnation of the person who first discovered the sacred herb, Ganja, many millennia ago. Bubba believed that once we die we return to the great milky sea of consciousness the Nagas churn, night and day, to create the material world we know and perceive. He believed that we come out of the milky sea when we are born and incarnate as humans to live our lives in this physical world. The world, in Bubba's beliefs, was here so that consciousness could experience material life.

Bubba believed in a moral code based on the well-known and simple golden rule: Treat others how you want to be treated. That, and remember you're going to come back again, so treat the world well.

Bubba believed that we have to repeat our incarnations until we have gained sufficient experience in our consciousness that we no longer need to reincarnate any further.

He believed that we make heaven or hell everyday in our own lives by the way we live, so he choose to live in a heavenly direction and encouraged his followers to do the same.

Bubba believed in the daily use of Ganja, the two-dog plant, for wisdom and well-being. He believed the Nommos had brought the plant to Earth as a part of their galaxy-wide project to take the herb to all inhabited planets. A noble project indeed! Bubba considered the act of growing Ganja as a way to live life in a heavenly direction.

Bubba believed George Van Tassel and what he had to say about the space brothers. He believed that many of the space brothers are currently living on the planet and he was pretty sure a few had come to the drum circles in the past. He believed in aliens from the Pleiades, from the Orion constellation, the Virgo Constellation and, of course, Sirius.

Bubba believed that Earth was, some how, in the whole

cosmic scheme of things, an important place. Where else could you see all the familiar constellations? Nowhere better than on Earth. Bubba had, of course, an Earth-centric view point. He wasn't aware of the strange and different constellations you can see from other star systems, but I'll let him slide on this one.

Then there were the Nagas. The Nagas didn't actually exist, physically, in his worldview, not really. They were mythical creatures, metaphors to describe the indescribable. They weren't supposed to show up at your camp in the desert. They were supposed to stay mythical creatures for Bubba to pepper his stories with around the drum circle. Most inconvenient, this arrival of the Nagas.

-48-

LEVELS

While we have our next smoke break, I think this would be a good moment in our story to discuss the different levels of the marijuana experience:

The first level is just getting high. This takes very little marijuana, a puff or two. Your head usually feels a little lighter than usual, in a good way, and your thoughts begin to run together. New ideas seem to suddenly occur to you. New smokers usually get the giggles because everything seems so darn funny when you're high.

The next level is stoned. Stoned is the feeling you get after smoking about a whole joint by yourself. What happens next depends on the pot you're smoking. If it's a Sativa you're probably going to want to get busy with some creative project. And I mean really involved in the project. If it's an Indica you're probably going to just want to chill somewhere and contemplate something, anything. The mind will journey and asks questions like a child, and usually comes up with really groovy answers.

The third level is couch-locked. Couch-lock comes after way too much pot smoking. This state is way beyond stoned and is that point when you are literally stuck on the couch, watching TV without the energy to move your finger on the remote. In this state nothing is going to get done except sleep, even getting up to get munchies is too much of an effort. It's a twilight state of mind where you drift in the void between sleep and wakefulness for an endless time before sleep finally takes over.

I don't know if there is a level that comes after couch-locked, because in that state it takes super-human willpower to get up the energy to smoke anymore pot.

If getting couch-locked is your goal when smoking the herb, and you smoke daily, your tolerance levels are going to go up a lot faster than a person who just gets high on the weekends.

Tolerance. One of the things that happens after you've been smoking the herb for a while is you start to develop a tolerance to the herb. What this means is that it takes more herb to get you high then it used to. This, of course, leads to the question, is this a good thing or a bad thing?

First off, building up a tolerance is a natural thing. It is the way the human body is built to process the cannabinoids in the herb, and the body does it well. Cannabinoids are the chemical compounds that cause the marijuana effects. After a person has been smoking a while, the body gets used to a certain level of cannabinoids in the system, and shuts down receptors in the brain to accept any more, even if they keep smoking. This mechanism in the body prevents marijuana from becoming toxic to the body system no matter how much herb a person smokes.

Research has shown that it takes two days for your receptors to return to their previous levels and around four weeks for them to return to normal. This is even if you smoked the proverbial pound of marijuana in one sitting.

Tolerance is often looked on as a negative thing, something you should avoid, but I'd like to suggest that it's actually a positive thing. It means that you can smoke the herb and still get stuff done. The visual and auditory side effects of herb smoking that happen at first could be distracting if they happened every time you smoked. Luckily your system gets used to the herb, quickly.

If building up a tolerance is bothersome there are several things you can do to fix the situation. You can avoid the tolerance factor a bit by cutting back on your pot smoking, switching to a different kind of pot, or by quitting for a while. It only takes a few weeks for the body to reset itself and to bring your tolerance levels back down to where they were when you first started smoking the herb.

Ffftzoit.

-49-
NAGA BAR

It took Dylan a while to recover from his time in the hospital. For a month he had to have Mel hook him up to an IV for a half hour every morning. Dylan had learned that being out of the hospital didn't mean he was well. Recovery was going to be a long road. The whole incident had put Dylan in a reflective mood about his life. He wondered what he believed.

Dylan had grown up a Christian and had gone to a private Christian high school. After high school, when he no longer had to go to church, he had stopped going for good. He didn't know if he really believed in Jesus once, or if he was just going along with what he was supposed to say back then. Having come so close to death made Dylan yearn to believe something, even if it was Christianity.

Dylan had quit smoking pot at this time and didn't know what he was going to do about that. He was a little leery about smoking again, at least so soon after the treatments. But he did miss the feeling of being high, after all, Dylan has been using the herb for nearly thirty-five years and he was more used to being high than he was being "normal".

Dylan went to his collective in Palm Springs to see what

they might have, some kind of edible or something he could use as a substitute for smoking. At the collective they had a new chocolate bar made from herb grown in the hi-desert called a Naga Bar. Dylan bought a couple and headed back home.

The chocolate tasted amazing. It was a sweet dark chocolate with a citrus flavor. Dylan didn't realize how far down his tolerance was when he first tried the chocolate and he ate too much. The chocolate took about forty-five minutes to kick in and then Dylan's world went sideways for a while. He had trouble walking because everything felt slanted at weird angles, so he sat, leaning, at the kitchen table waiting for the feeling to pass, which it did after an hour. Soon the effects mellowed to a point where Dylan could enjoy the ride.

The next day Dylan tried a smaller piece of chocolate and had a great time. His body loved feeling the herb again. It was like being back home.

After a month, when the IVs were done with, and the PICC line had been removed, Dylan tried smoking again. Mel knew he would.

-50-

HEART SICK

Mitch was sick after his road rage incident. Darlene couldn't get him to talk about it. As usual, after he lost his temper he felt sick to his heart and the sickness spread throughout his body. They found a place to camp for the night at a KOA near Flagstaff, Arizona, and Mitch went to bed in the back of the RV.

The next day Mitch was sick - shaking, with a slight fever, and stayed in bed most of the day. Darlene kept checking on Mitch, thinking that they should find an emergency room but Mitch insisted that he'd be okay in a few days. Darlene tried to busy herself around the RV. She was concerned.

After a couple of days Mitch finally apologized about the incident. He explained how he had a problem with that behind the wheel. Usually smoking the herb helped keep it from happening but every so often he felt this mood settle on him for a few days and he'd start having trouble sleeping. Then some little thing would set him off and he couldn't think straight. He would see red and something usually ended up broken. And then he'd get sick. Sometimes he even ended up in the hospital because he got so sick.

Darlene listened to Mitch and adjusted to the new reality.

"This just happens in the car?" asked Darlene.

"Not always, I've smashed a few windows and broken a few phones," replied Mitch, feeling glad to have someone to talk to about this problem.

"Okay, how do we keep this from happening? Obviously it makes you sick and it freaked me out."

"I'll let you know when I feel the strange mood hit me," suggested Mitch.

"Let's start there," said Darlene.

-51-

RETURNING TO NAGALAND

Dylan and Mel saw a flier for the Nagaland drum circle while getting coffee at a local coffee shop. The flier had the same seven-headed cobra logo as the chocolates Dylan had been buying. It peaked their interest and they decided to check out the next drum circle, which was coming up that weekend.

Bubba Ravi Shesha had returned to Nagaland after a two-week retreat. The Naganites were overjoyed to have their leader back. Everything had been running smoothly while he was gone, thanks to Melissa Kingsnake. No more Nagas had shown up since that night several weeks earlier.

Augustus was doing wonders with the chocolate Naga Bar brand. He had found a manufacturer who was able to use all their trimmings to make high quality chocolates. The chocolates had sold out at collectives around Palm Springs and the rest of the low-desert, shortly after the brand was launched.

It had been good for Bubba to take a break but he wasn't any closer to figuring out what to do about the Nagas. He had reviewed his beliefs numerous times and found little he disagreed with or needed to change. It was a work in progress at this point but it wasn't going to stop him for being the spiritual leader of the twenty-two Naganites and the many assorted visitors to Nagaland. *There are appearances to keep up until this soul-searching is done*, thought Bubba.

The drum circle and vegetarian feast that weekend was for the full moon and it would be Bubba's celebration of ending his fast. Bubba hadn't eaten solid food or smoked Ganja for over two weeks. He had been drinking only juices and water. After all, Bubba wasn't joking around. He really needed some answers to his questions about the Nagas.

When Dylan and Mel arrived on Saturday evening, they were impressed by the large feast that had been laid out by the Naganites. Mel loved vegetarian food, Dylan not so much. Dylan preferred a nice juicy hamburger but was pleasantly surprised when he tried Sandy's portobello mushroom burger.

Before the drum circle began Dylan asked around about the chocolates and was introduced to Augustus. The two hit it off and Augustus ended up getting out some chocolates for whoever wanted to try them.

Bubba slowly started on the food. He didn't want to rush into eating after fasting for several weeks. Mostly he ate melons. Dylan and Mel had no idea that Bubba was going through a soul-searching period, nothing about him showed it. He was his usual, jovial self, glad it was a full moon and time for a drum circle.

The drum circle began at dusk, about fifteen minutes before the moon would rise over the mesas to the east. The hymns to the Nagas began shortly after the moon appeared. Tonight the didgeridoo players had been joined by a keyboard player who added ethereal sounds to the musical mix. Augustus and the joint rolling team started sending joints around the circle as Randy Rattlesnake lit the fire in the pit.

For forty-five minutes the drumming continued, sometimes waning, sometimes growing to a powerful rumbling beat. Dylan had brought a drum along and joined in with the circle. Several of the Naganites had gotten up and were dancing away under the full moon light. Karina performed an amazing fire dance.

As you can imagine, deep underground the Nagas heard the pounding of the drums and the music and started towards the surface again. This time a dozen Nagas were headed towards Nagaland. They wanted to see who was creating this interesting music. And because Nagas travel really fast, when they want to, they were soon hidden among the boulders before the first round of drumming came to an end.

-52-

LET'S GO TO JOSHUA TREE

There weren't anymore incidents of road rage on the way back to Long Beach. Mitch was on his best behavior and soon the incident was mostly forgotten.

It was good to be back home again. Mitch's cats were about as thrilled as cats get when Mitch and Darlene returned home. John was glad to see them again. They had so many photos and stories to share.

The big question that Mitch and Darlene kept returning to was where to make a home, where to buy, or build a house. Both Mitch and Darlene liked the mountains and lots of trees, but that's not where they felt like living. As they had been traveling they had been keeping their eyes open for a place to settle down.

Within a few days of being home, Mitch had completely cleaned up Lucky, and the RV was looking good as new. That got the two thinking about where to go next, itching to be back on the road. Darlene had watched a video online about Joshua Tree National Park and thought that might make a nice week-long trip.

Darlene brought up the idea while they were hanging out with John smoking a joint.

"I love Joshua Tree," said John excitedly when Darlene brought up the idea.

"Really? Why?" asked Mitch.

"Have you ever been there?" John asked. Joshua Tree was the only National Park he had traveled to as a child, and enjoyed. Just the name Joshua Tree brought back fond memories.

"No."

"Well, it isn't like desert you see in movies with just sand and dunes. It's got lots of life, interesting boulders and dark skies at night. It's just two hours away and it's a whole other world."

"I'd love to go see it," said Darlene.

"I'd love to go with you two, if that's okay?" asked John.

"Sure, let's do it." said Mitch, finalizing the idea.

"Can we go tomorrow?" asked Darlene.

Mitch looked at John who nodded his head yes.

"We'll leave in the morning." said Mitch.

The rest of the evening was spent preparing for the next day's trip.

The three of them got on the freeway around 9:00 the next morning. Darlene had booked a site in a private campground in North Joshua Tree because they had read that the park was almost constantly full and it was hard to get camping spots. The traffic was still bad from the morning rush hour but they weren't in any hurry. John, who played guitar, strummed a bunch of different songs while they waited through the traffic. It was a beautiful Spring morning and all the hills were green from the recent rains.

After a couple of hours the traffic melted away and Lucky was cruising through open hills near Beaumont, the road trip was really underway. Soon they passed a freeway sign that said "other Desert Cities" and John said they were almost to highway 62. Highway 62 takes you from the main interstate, the 10, to Joshua Tree and other desert cities.

Within forty-five minutes the three of them were pulling into the parking lot at the Joshua Tree Saloon, where they stopped to get their bearings and stretch their legs. The Joshua Tree Saloon is a great place to stop and stretch your legs. They serve good food and the service is always friendly. Just saying.

After a nice lunch, Mitch, Darlene and John got back on the road and headed towards North Joshua Tree to get their camping spot before they went and explored the National Park. The campsite they got was really private and run by a young couple who lived on site. There was a nice, level area to park Lucky with an amazing view of the Morongo Basin, all the way to the National Park.

Mitch was impressed with the hi-desert and the view from their site. The three of them set up camp and relaxed, smoked a joint and enjoyed the scenery. The afternoon turned into late afternoon, 4:20 came and went and Mitch kept remarking about how much he liked it here. John kept saying "you haven't seen anything yet". Darlene kept repeating how nice it all was.

Later, after burgers had been cooked over the open fire and enjoyed, the three sat around the fire pit and talked for hours. It was a full moon night and the desert was lit up like a second sunrise of moon glow.

"What is it about a fire in the desert?" asked Mitch after the conversation had gotten quiet. "It like you expect the voice of God to come out the flames."

"Yeah..." Darlene and John said in unison.

-53-

A TOUGH REPORT

The Nommos were camping out too, on the dark side of the moon. Their ships were docked at an ancient and abandoned space port that was littered with Orionite graffiti. The Orionites, gangsters from Orion, left graffiti everywhere they went throughout the galaxy. The Nommos were working on their report for the home office about the state of life and the herb on planet Earth. The report wasn't looking good.

There was so much pollution now, many wars and continuous acts of violence all over the Earth. Large areas of the forests, the lungs of the planet, had been clear cut, and replaced by crops watered with pesticides. Plastics had inundated the oceans and were choking out much of the sea life. Plant and animal species were diminishing across the globe at a terrifying rate.

As for the herb - the sacred herb had been banned worldwide for decades. Some people had spent ten to twenty years in prison just for possessing the plant. This, of course, was done on purpose for a number of nefarious reasons, usually involving politics, ignorance, greed or stupidity.

Whatever people were in charge of the planet were doing a

fine job of fucking it up for years to come. And that wasn't even considering the nuclear weapons and waste. The Nommos were coming close to suggesting a reset for planet Earth but they took into account that we are in the late Kali Yuga and things should be in bad shape at this time.

Tough report, man. Time for a smoke break.

-54-
PEEK BEHIND THE CURTAIN

While we enjoy another joint of this fine marijuana I've been smoking, let's take a peek behind the writing curtain...

Have you ever thought about words and what a miracle they are? I think about it often. I consider it a miracle that I can think a thought in my head, write it down using words, which are a combination of twenty-six different symbols, and you, possibly thousands of miles away can read my words and have my thoughts in your head.

There was once a time when humankind did not know about the possibility of using written words. To communicate over a long distance you had to tell a person your message. They would have to memorize your message, run wherever you intended your message to go and deliver it. What a hassle. But humankind did this for thousands of years.

Then along came Odin, the Norse god, who hung himself upside down on a tree for nine days. For doing this feat he was rewarded with the knowledge of The Runes, or how to make words. And here we are, many millennia down the road and for the most part we've lost the magic of what it means to be able to put words on paper. There is a reason they call it spelling, because it’s a form of magic, it’s the ability to cast a spell over someone's mind.

So here we are, way deep into this novel, constructed out of words. All of these words are just thoughts in my head. Someone like Dylan only exists inside the words of this story, and now he exists in your thoughts. This is because Dylan is just information and energy. He solidly exists in my imagination and as a transmitter of information and energy, I am able to send that information and energy to you, who are able to receive that through my words. Depending on how well our imaginations work together, the story comes to life. Magic, if you ask me.

To look at it from another perspective, a bigger perspective – you and I are information and energy. We are information and energy brought to life by the stories we live out and these stories are expressions of our consciousness and imagination.

Ffftzoit.

-55-

AT THE DRUM CIRCLE

In Nagaland, the second round of the drum circle was beginning. Deep in the boulders were a dozen Nagas, watching. The moon had risen, and the full moon was lighting up the desert in an otherworldly glow. The light from the fire cast strange dancing shadows across the boulders. The Nagas swayed to the rhythm of the drums, deep in the shadows where they couldn't be seen.

Dylan and Mel were both pretty stoned by this point and were grooving on the sound textures of the synth player, the didgeridoos and the drums. Soon a number of people were up and moving to the beat, including Dylan and Mel.

The Nagas wanted to join the people dancing around the fire but knew they couldn't, they knew they were not allowed to interact with humans, a strict Naga law. Once their curiosity was satisfied, the Nagas returned to their underground world before they could be discovered. Unfortunately, the Nagas left before Bubba Ravi Shesha took center stage and began his story for the evening.

"Reality," began Bubba, "what is it? Is it real? How much of it is real? How much of reality do we even know about?"

The music had quieted down to one drummer and the synth player.

"What is behind the reality we experience every day? Is reality an illusion as many traditions tell us? I have been asking myself these questions over the last few weeks. I've been asking myself a lot of questions, about everything I believe. I ask myself, what is belief and what do I really know from experience? I don't have interest in beliefs anymore. I want to know what is real."

More joints passed around the circle, Bubba took a hit when the first one came by and said, "Om, Yummie Yummie.

"What are beliefs anyway? Mostly they're just things we've heard about and never experienced ourselves. That's second-hand information, at best. Who needs second-hand information? Once you've experienced something you have knowledge, mostly incomplete knowledge, but first-hand knowledge all the same. That's what I'm looking for. That's what I want us to be able to experience here in Nagaland, experiences that lead to first-hand knowledge. If our beliefs don't agree with our experiences of reality, then our beliefs have to go. We need pragmatic beliefs.

"Now, you might be wondering, especially our guests, why I'm questioning my beliefs, why I'm putting them to the test. We had an interesting thing happen here a couple of weeks ago. We were visited by actual, real-live Nagas. They were about fifteen feet long and three of them were captured on security video tape."

The crowd around the fire pit broke up into hushed conversations. The Naganites were surprised Bubba had said anything and the guests were amazed at this news.

"Now, I've been talking about Nagas for years. I've also been talking about the Space Brothers for years, about the Venusians and the Pleiadians. I never expected any of them to show up, to actually show up. And now the Nagas have shown up. We have first-hand evidence of these ancient creatures, it's not just a mystical belief we hold. And this is the difference between belief and knowledge. To tell you the truth, it's shaken my world."

Bubba made a hand gesture that meant the drum circle should begin again. It was an incredibly short talk for Bubba. He had cut his talk short because he had surprised himself by what he said. The Ganja must have been stronger than he was expecting. What Bubba had said was what was laying heavy on his mind. It forced its way out.

After the second round of the drum circle, everyone enjoyed another round of the vegetarian feast. And then one last round of the drum circle for the evening.

Dylan and Mel introduced themselves to Bubba after the drumming was done. Dylan was curious about the Nagas he had mentioned briefly.

"Yeah, our security cameras captured footage of them slithering around the camp," Bubba told them.

"Wow, that's incredible. Is there anyway we can see the footage?"

"We're going to have a talk on the Nagas in two weeks, at our next drum circle, we're going to show some footage then."

"We'll be here."

-56-

HOUSE HUNTING

Mitch fell in love with the hi-desert. It does that to some people. From morning to bed time he found things to love about the desert.

"Wouldn't it be nice to have a place out here?" Mitch asked Darlene one morning after they had been camping for several days. Mitch had been thinking about it a lot. If he had to have a house somewhere this would be a sweet place.

"I love it here too, but it is spring. I understand it gets intensely hot during the summer," replied Darlene.

"Then we travel to somewhere cooler if it gets too hot," Mitch was really getting excited at the thought of having a desert home. "We can travel anywhere from here and not have to start out in two hours of traffic."

"You can only move if you have a guest room, so I can come and stay," interjected John.

"But, of course!" replied Mitch.

The trip morphed into a house-hunting adventure. They drove into Joshua Tree and had a little breakfast at The Crossroads Cafe, so they could get a WiFi connection. Mitch was amazed at the prices of houses after scanning through some listings on his iPad.

“Oh, man, we can buy just about any house we want, and with land! These prices are great,” said Mitch, “We could get a place with about 10 acres and grow some great pot,” Mitch was sold on the idea of moving to the hi-desert, and now his mind was racing with ideas.

“Let’s find a real estate agent and go look at houses,” said Darlene, getting into the spirit of the adventure.

“Yes, let’s,” agreed John.

Before breakfast was over they had contacted a local real estate agent named Bill Smith who had a bunch of good reviews online. Bill suggested they meet at his office, and he’d take them around to a few different listings.

The rest of the day was spent looking at four different desert houses. Bill assured them that if they didn’t find what they were looking for today, then he’d be watching the local real estate market everyday to help them find the perfect place. Mitch and Darlene were having a ball knowing they could buy any of the houses they looked at. John, who just liked looking at houses for the fun of it, was enjoying imagining visiting Mitch and Darlene at each place they went.

The last place they looked at was in North Joshua Tree, near the private campground where they were staying. It was a rambling ranch house on ten acres. There was a place to park an RV next to the house. There were several out-buildings, a huge garage and a barn. The land had once been a horse property and still had stables and corrals. There was also about an acre that had several green houses.

Darlene fell in love with the inside of the house, especially the kitchen. The kitchen was big and open and had a breakfast booth in corner with a view looking out over Morongo Basin towards the park. The house had five bedrooms and a huge living room with a large stone fireplace.

“If we lived here we’d need to get a dog or two to help us fill up the place,” said Mitch, imagining the possibilities.

"And maybe a horse," joked Darlene.

"Yeah, maybe a horse." replied Mitch, lost in thought.

The house had been on the market for a just few days and was listed for a reasonable price. Bill Smith pointed out numerous details about the house and the land, like the fact that the house had a new roof, and a well on the land, as well as city water in the main house.

"A well?" asked Mitch.

"Yup. Out by the greenhouses," answered Bill.

After a while they had thoroughly looked the place over and everyone gathered on the front porch. The porch wrapped all the way around the house. From the front porch they had the same view across the basin as the kitchen.

"What a great view," said John, "it's just like our campsite."

"What do you think, Darlene, I think I love the place. Listen to the quiet," said Mitch.

Everyone stood still and listened to the quiet.

"It sure feels nice here," replied Darlene.

"I think I could spend a lot of time here," said Mitch.

Mitch and Darlene wandered around again and talked it over. They were both sold on the place. There were a few little things that needed fixing but only minor things. The price was, as I mentioned, reasonable, so they decided to take the place at the offered price.

Bill Smith called the agent representing the sellers and told her about the offer the Hopewells wanted to make on the house. No one else had made a bid on the house yet, so it looked good.

"We should know by tomorrow morning if they accept your offer," said Bill.

It was late afternoon by the time Bill drove them back to his office so they could get their RV.

"Well that was fast," remarked John as they drove back to their campsite.

"I sure hope we get the place," said Darlene.

“Me too,” said Mitch.

That evening around the campfire was full of talk about the house and the land. All three of them had taken photos with their phones and they kept passing their photos around the fire showing off different aspects of the house and land.

“I was serious about getting a dog or two,” said Mitch.

“I love dogs,” replied Darlene. They smiled at each other. They both had that inner excitement that comes from buying a house and all the possibilities ahead.

The next morning Bill called them before they had even had coffee. The seller had accepted their offer! Mitch and Darlene were ecstatic.

-57-

GOLDENSNAKE

Louie traveled back and forth between Long Beach and Nagaland nearly every weekend. Karina was staying with the Naganites and that was one of the main attractions for him, but he had also become good friends with Tony Mamba. Louie, it turned out, was a pretty good drummer and enjoyed participating in the drum circle. The thing that really brought Louie out to the desert each weekend was a chance to spend time in the Ganja garden.

Several times Bubba had asked Louie if he wanted to join the Naganites and work full time in the garden, but so far Louie had turned down the offer. He was wary about joining a cult. He had seen the video of the Nagas and wasn't sure he felt like venerating them. But slowly Louie was warming up to the idea of the cult. He enjoyed the feeling of community the cult provided, it was becoming like a family to him.

Louie spent a whole work week thinking about making the move to Nagaland. Jesus & Jesus had been good to him and given him a chance when no one else would. He liked his studio apartment and his independence. He didn't have much to give the cult when, and if, he joined but that didn't matter too much. After a week of thinking about it seriously Louie had run out of reasons not to join up and all he could think of was reasons to become a Naganite. That weekend he asked Bubba if he could become a member of the cult.

The Naganites were thrilled to have Louie join their cult and held a special ceremony that included a huge two-day feast and a drum circle session to welcome him into their group. Bubba gave Louie his new last name, Goldensnake, and gave him his sacred mantra, which is secret, so I can't share it with you. Karina did an extra special fire dance during the drum circle in honor of Louie.

Karina was planning on returning to Oregon but kept postponing the trip because of Louie. Bubba had asked her many times to join the cult and stay for good but Karina was too much of a gypsy to settle down, or at least that's the way it had always been in the past. But now that Louie had joined the cult she was re-thinking her decision. She believed in following her heart and her heart was falling in love with Louie Goldensnake.

-58-

OPEN TO THE PUBLIC

Now that Bubba had let the news of the Nagas visit out of the bag, the Naganites had decided to go public with their videos. At the next drum circle Bubba was going to give a talk about the Nagas and show the video. They knew things were going to change after the next drum circle, so they wanted it to be the best one ever. It was going to be a new moon night and the desert would be enveloped in darkness.

The Naganites put up fliers all over the hi-desert, at coffee shops and little businesses, announcing the next drum circle and vegetarian feast, with a special talk by Bubba Ravi Shesha about the mysterious Nagas.

Mitch, Darlene and John saw one of the fliers when they were getting lunch at a local coffee shop called Frontier.

"Look at this," John said, pointing to the flier, "You want to come back in two weeks? This looks interesting."

"Nagaland… where have I heard that name?" asked Mitch.

A little while later, while eating, Mitch remembered where he had seen the name Nagaland.

"They grow pot at Nagaland. Really good stuff I understand," said Mitch, "I saw an article in *Culture Magazine* about the place a couple of months ago."

John had just been looking up Nagaland on his phone.

"They're only fifteen miles away and the place is open to the public," reported John.

"Let's go check out Nagaland," suggested Darlene.

"Let's do it," said Mitch.

The drive out to Nagaland went up through Pioneertown and along a beautiful stretch of hi-desert.

"Maybe we should buy a place up here too," said Mitch, only half-joking.

There was a big open gate with a huge sign over it that said Nagaland in large metal letters. That was a new addition to the place, thanks to Augustus' recent contribution.

The three of them were met by Melissa when they pulled up to the compound.

"You can camp over there," she said, pointing to the camping area, "we have free WiFi now."

"We came for the tour," said John, who had gotten out of the RV. "Is there a tour?"

"Oh, a tour?" answered Melissa, confused.

"I read online that Nagaland was open to the public, so I assumed there was a tour. Do you have a gift shop?"

"No, we don't have a gift shop, but that's not a bad idea. And we don't have a tour either, but I can show you around."

Melissa showed them around the compound where they got to meet a number of Naganites and Bubba Ravi Shesha. Bubba and a few Naganites had just lit a fat joint and were passing it around, Mitch, Darlene and John were happy to join in the session.

"Ffftzoit," said Mitch, thinking about the Waldos for some reason.

"Om, Yummie Yummie," said Bubba.

-59-

PAINTING NAGAS

Mitch, Darlene and John were enchanted by their visit to Nagaland and with the Naganites. Mitch bought several ounces of pot from the Naganites and a dozen Naga Bars before they left. Bubba had told them a little about the Naga sighting, just enough to make sure they would come back for the drum circle.

"Wow, that place was cool," remarked John as soon as they were back inside the RV, "I'm coming back whether you guys come or not."

"I think we'll be back," said Mitch.

"I liked that Bubba," said Darlene, she didn't clarify if she meant the person or the herb.

Mitch drove them all back to the campsite for their last night in Joshua Tree, for now.

Meanwhile, Dylan and Melanie were sitting on their patio, looking out over the basin, at the cars flowing along the highway. If they were using binoculars they would have seen Mitch, Darlene and John driving along in Lucky the RV.

Dylan had eaten a piece of a Naga Bar an hour earlier and was starting to feel the effects. He and Mel were passing a joint back and forth.

"Om, Yummie Yummie," said Dylan, imitating Bubba's voice.

Mel laughed and took a hit, "Om, Yummie Yummie."

Both of them had a great time at Nagaland and had been talking about it much of the afternoon. Dylan had looked up Nagas on the computer and found out all kinds of information about the mythical serpent people. He learned about their Hindu history and how Shesha was asked by the Brahma to carry the world in his dreaded hair. He learned about how the Nagas had stirred the milky oceans of creation and helped create the world. He learned that Nagas are extremely handsome creatures but can be dangerous to other species because their bite is poisonous.

"I'm thinking about painting some Nagas," said Dylan, who had his sketch book out and was beginning to make some preliminary drawings.

"I imagine they'd look pretty cool," replied Mel, who was Dylan's biggest fan.

"Let's go down to the studio in a while," suggested Dylan.

"Sure. I'll make us some sandwiches for later," agreed Mel. She loved to sit in the studio and watch Dylan paint. Forms would magically appear on the canvas as the vision in Dylan's mind would start to be revealed.

Dylan's studio was in a store front in downtown Joshua Tree. He had about two thousand square feet of space to work in and sometimes worked on very large canvases. When Dylan started on a new idea he liked to begin with a 24" x 36" canvas. After several weeks or months, as his ideas took larger form, he would graduate to bigger canvases.

The studio was furnished with several old sofas and a number of rugs on the floor. There were two swamp coolers to keep the place cool in the summer and a wood burning stove to keep it warm in the winter. Soon Mel was stretched out on one of the sofas where she could watch the work develop. Dylan was already sketching with pencil on a canvas, and was ready to begin painting.

-60-

MYSTERIOUS FORCES

The Nommos had completed their report for the home office and were going to relax a little before heading back home. Like everyone else in our story, they headed to Joshua Tree.

In their report the situation on the planet was painted in desperate colors. If it weren't for the fact that the world was on the cusp of a new Golden Age, they would have called for a full reset of the planet. Of course, moving out of the Kali Yuga into the new Satya Yuga, or Golden Age, would cause a full reset on its own, so the Nommos opted to let time take its course. They'd be back in a thousand years to help humanity pick up the pieces and carry on.

Mitch, Darlene and John had driven back to Long Beach, and couldn't wait to get back to the hi-desert. The house was in escrow now but that should go quickly. Mitch and Darlene needed to drive up to Washington to get some of Darlene's things but they were going to wait until after the next drum circle. John was thinking about selling his apartment buildings and moving out to Joshua Tree too, he had really gotten caught up in the excitement.

Augustus Cobra and Sandy Cornsnake were an item now.

Things had gotten interesting at Nagaland with the changes going on with Bubba. Bubba was still questioning his beliefs to figure out what was authentic and what was just bullshit he had picked up over the years. A few disillusioned Naganites had left the cult. Bubba sent each one off with an ounce of pot, a pocketful of cash and a thank you for participating in their social experiment.

Most of the remaining Naganites were busy with the plans for the next drum circle. The footage of the Nagas had been made into several YouTube videos with narrations by Bubba. They were going to post the videos on the day after the new moon. The drum circle members were practicing everyday to make this the best drum circle ever. Sandy and the feast preparation team were expecting a larger than usual crowd for the upcoming gathering.

Dylan and Mel were both looking forward to the next drum circle with anticipation. Dylan had been working on a new series of paintings inspired by the Nagas and he couldn't wait to see the videos. In his paintings, the Nagas were attacking people. He had completed several canvases already and they reflected some anxiety and confusion about this ancient race of creatures.

Meanwhile, in the background of reality the mysterious forces of information, energy, and consciousness were at work to bring all these people together around the drum circle. Why? I don't know yet. These forces seemed to have their own plans for that evening, and they usually has the last say on things like these.

-61-

JUST CARRY ON

I've been writing steadily for several weeks now and my baggie of pot is getting near the bottom. Let's see if I can stretch it out to make it to the end of the story. I kind of wish I had some of that Nagaland pot, maybe some of the Bubba Kush, and possibly a Naga Bar or two.

As it stands, I figure I've got enough herb left to smoke for a couple more days before I'm going to have to re-up. I'm hunkered down for the completion of this story. I've got food supplies and I can put off my other work for a couple of days. There are more important things at hand, like smoking a bowl and finding out what happens next.

For the last several days I've been waiting to see where this story is going. I figure the story already exists somewhere in our collective consciousness, in the aether. Much of the story has written itself. I've just been watching what's going on and writing it down. Each piece has come to me as I needed it and now I find myself trying to look further than the next page to guess why Dylan, Mel, Mitch, Darlene, John, Bubba, Melissa, Augustus, Sandy, Louie, Karina and the Naganites are going to be at the drum circle coming up in a week. Of course, it's entirely possible that the drum circle isn't the point but only a moment in the story and the end of the story is far beyond the edge of the horizon. We will find out soon enough.

I'd like to note that this story has moved along so quickly, I don't want it to end anytime soon. So I hope you don't mind me trying to stretch it out a bit further. I drew an *Oblique Strategy* card today with the question in my mind of where this story should go next and the card said "Just Carry On". The card made me laugh. Then I drew a second card for clarification and that card said, "Try and do nothing for as long as possible". So there's that.

As I was saying, this book already exists out there in the aether and I just need to discover how it ends. Anything and everything that has been and will be created by humans exists in the collective consciousness, in the aether. I'm sure the cure for cancer exists out there, just waiting for someone to tune into it. This is where intuition comes into play. I've been following my intuition throughout this story, that's how I can see what's going on at any moment. Of course, this does lead to the question of how everything is out there in collective consciousness in the first place.

If you can imagine this: my whole life, and everyone's life, all of our collective consciousness is like this book. Everything that exists is in this book, and the book is already written and being added to at the same time. The whole book exists but you can only read one page at a time. The page you're reading is the present, the pages you've already read are the past and what's left to read is the future. At any moment, if you have the ability, you can access any information in this book by turning to the right page. But I digress.

Ffftzoit. Back to the story.

-62-

HI-DESERT DREAMING

Now that he had traveled a bit John was getting tired of life in Long Beach. He wasn't sure what to do about it yet, but there was a growing desire to sell the apartment buildings and follow Mitch and Darlene to the hi-desert. John had lived his whole life in Long Beach, so this would be a big change. Something inside was nudging him to follow through on the feeling.

John ordered a number of books about the Mojave desert and Joshua Tree: geology books, stars viewing guides, and anything he could to keep his thoughts on the hi-desert while he went through his daily life as a building owner, with sinks to unclog and toilets to unplug. John had tacked a big map of Joshua Tree National Park on his wall to help keep him focused on the growing plan.

Mitch and Darlene had been packing up the apartment. They were going to hire movers do the actual moving but Mitch was particular and wanted to pack up everything himself. The cats were upset and bothered by all the stuff being moved around.

There was a calendar hanging on the kitchen wall of Mitch's apartment. Darlene checked of each day as they looked forward to returning to the hi-desert. The house was proceeding through escrow and there had been a number of issues that had to be dealt with, house inspectors to hire, etc.. The Realtor, Bill Smith, was taking care of most of the little issues that came up concerning the house.

In the evenings the three of them would get together, have a smoke, and share what little bits of information they had learned about the desert that day.

"How long do you want to stay in Joshua Tree, when we go up this week?" Darlene asked Mitch and John one evening.

"As long as you guys want," said John.

"We have to have the house inspected and we want to be there for that, so I was thinking about going up a little early," said Mitch.

"I could be ready to go as soon as tomorrow, if you like," said John.

"Let's hit the road the day after tomorrow if we can get that spot at the private campground again," suggested Darlene.

"Great, let's do it," said Mitch, "but let's leave around noon and avoid as much morning traffic as we can."

-63-

HOME INSPECTION

It was Wednesday afternoon before Mitch, Darlene and John got on the road. The traffic was relatively clear and within two and a half hours they were pulling into the private campsite in North Joshua Tree. They had plenty of time to set up their camp before 4:20. The young couple that owned the campsite came by for a visit and shared a joint with them at the magical time.

They were smoking some of the Nagaland Bubba Kush and it was fantastic. Mitch had been smoking nothing but Bubba Kush since they returned from the hi-desert. Even though Mitch had an incredible tolerance to the herb, this Bubba Kush had a way of really getting him stoned every time.

Mitch, Darlene and John all had a certain excitement from returning to a place they had been to recently. Everything was still new but not like seeing it for their first time. Most of the businesses they re-visited remembered them from just a couple of weeks ago. They were getting a taste of being locals, and it felt good. They felt like they belonged there in the hi-desert.

The house inspection was scheduled for Friday morning and the drum circle was on Saturday night, so they had a little time on their hands. They drove out to Wonder Valley, east of Joshua

Tree, on Thursday afternoon and eventually ended up at a little roadhouse called The Palms. It was late by the time they got back to the campsite and everyone was tired but excited about the house inspection the next day. Mitch and Darlene hadn't seen the house since the first day they looked at it.

The three of them woke up early the next morning. They made a quick breakfast and drove off to visit the house. Mitch and Darlene were a bit concerned it wouldn't be as great as they remembered it.

Bill Smith met them at the house. Mitch and Darlene were relieved. It was just as nice as they remembered. The house inspectors, a couple, showed up after a while. They got to work immediately and Mitch and Darlene had to hurry to keep up with them. They went over everything from the foundation to the top of the roof, from plumbing to electricity. After three hours of going over the house with a fine tooth comb the inspectors only found two electrical plugs that didn't work. The house checked out.

After Bill Smith and the house inspectors left, Mitch, Darlene and John smoked a joint on the front porch to celebrate. If everything went right they would be returning in two weeks to get the keys.

-64-

NEW MOON DRUM CIRCLE

Dylan designed a Naga t-shirt and got it screen-printed in time for the drum circle. Both Dylan and Mel were wearing their Naga t-shirts when they went to the feast on Saturday night. The black t-shirt featured a seven-headed cobra printed in gold. He had several dozen t-shirts in the trunk of their car, just in case.

Mitch saw the Naga t-shirt on Dylan and Mel when they arrived shortly after the Winslows.

"Where did you get the Naga t-shirt?" asked Mitch as a way of introducing himself.

"I made it." answered Dylan.

"It's really cool. I love the style of the design," responded Mitch.

"I have some extras in my car if you want one."

"I'd love one, how much?"

"$20."

"I'll buy three right now."

"Great!"

Dylan and Mitch went over to Dylan's car to get the shirts.

"My name is Dylan, Dylan Winslow," said Dylan as he stretched out his hand to Mitch.

"Mitch Hopewell."

They shook hands.

"Those are some nice dreads you have," commented Mitch.

"Thanks," replied Dylan, "I've been growing them for eight years."

"You live around here?" Mitch asked Dylan as he was getting the shirts out of the trunk.

"Yeah, over near Joshua Tree. We love it. I mean my wife, Melanie, and I love it."

"Cool. We're buying a house in North Joshua Tree right now," said Mitch.

"Do you already live up here?"

"No, we live in Long Beach."

"Well, welcome to the hi-desert," said Dylan, he shook Mitch's hand again.

"Thanks, glad to be here."

Mitch took the t-shirts and went to the RV to change.

Meanwhile, Darlene introduced herself to Melanie. John had gone off to look for Augustus and found him with the joint rolling team. John joined in and rolled up a few joints for the evening ahead. Darlene and Melanie hit it off right away. Before long Darlene was showing Mel photos on her phone of their new house.

"Maybe we'll have a house warming," said Darlene enthusiastically.

"We'd love to come," replied Melanie.

Dylan and Mitch joined them, and the group sat together during the feast. John showed up after a bit. He had just smoked a joint with the joint rolling team and was ready to eat.

Sandy and the food preparation team had out done themselves. The feast was over the top. Over sixty guests had shown up and everyone ate until they were stuffed. There was still enough for everyone to have seconds or thirds.

The sun set during the feast and Randy Rattlesnake lit the

evening fire. Gradually everyone migrated to the fire pit where the drum circle had already congregated. The drumming began simply, with a focused intent. The drummers were determined to make this a memorable night.

Boom-badda-boom, boom-badda-boom, the drums began. There were two synth players tonight and they began with soft pads of ambient sound. The didgeridoo players joined in and the music increased in complexity. The sounds bounced off of the boulders around them and echoed back adding a nice delay effect.

Deep underground, the sound once again reached the ears of the curious Nagas and a small group of them headed towards the surface.

A number of joints started to be passed among the seated guests. Dylan had joined the circle of drummers and blended right into the rhythm. Karina the Fire Dreamer danced around spinning intricate patterns in the air with her fire pots. There was a sweet vibe running through all the people gathered at Nagaland. The frequencies of the sounds, the sweet herb, and the new moon vibrations all came together to create an amazing moment for everyone involved.

-65-

MEN-IN-BLACK

The vibe wasn't quite the same elsewhere in the hi-desert. A small team of Men-in-Black had gathered in Yucca Valley, and were now meeting with the local sheriff to find out all he knew about the folks out at Nagaland. The sheriff wasn't too happy about these strange outsiders nosing around his jurisdiction.

Men-in-Black (MiB) are part of the underground, super-secret government that operates in the shadows. The MiB police the many various species of aliens we have on this planet. Some aliens are multi-dimensional and terrestrial, but many had come from other planets, like the Nommos. Most people never have to deal with the MiB, but then again, most people aren't interacting with alien species either.

Nagaland had shown up on the radar of the MiB after Bubba had spilled the beans about the Nagas at the last drum circle. Word had quickly spread about the arrival of real-life Nagas. The former Naganites who had left the cult had already been picked up by the MiB for questioning.

The MiB planned to make a raid on the Naganite compound later that evening. They had contacted the DEA, and told them to raid the Naganites' completely legal marijuana grow that same night. They were going to use the DEA raid as cover for their own. The DEA wasn't too happy about that idea, but they had little choice. The MiB outranked the DEA. Tensions were high among the assembled teams from the different agencies.

The MiB team had dealt with Nagas before, so they were pretty sure what to expect. They didn't know if they would encounter the Nagas, but there was always that possibility. They were going in prepared for anything, as usual.

-66-

RUN THE VIDEO

The drumming continued for an hour before it quieted down to one drummer, a guy named Flynn Copperhead, who was a master of rhythm. Bubba stood up and walked slowly around the circle. There was a large screen set up on one side of the circle. A video started to play.

"This was recorded over a month ago with our security cameras," began Bubba.

The video showed three Nagas slithering out of the dark up to the gate of the compound.

"One of our security team saw these creatures in real life. We estimate that each of these creatures is over fifteen feet long. These creatures are called Nagas and they were written about many millennia ago by the Hindu writers of sacred literature. Supposedly, according to modern science, these creatures don't exist, but they do exist, just look," and with that Bubba gestured to the screen.

Flynn kept a steady beat going that matched the rhythm of the Nagas slithering around on the screen.

"Nagas are who we venerate here at Nagaland. We have written hymns to the Nagas and have held numerous drum circles to send our rhythms to them, apparently they have heard us. We had a drum circle the night the Nagas arrived, so we think it's the drums that have drawn the Nagas to the surface. We have searched around but haven't found any openings to the underworld of the Nagas. Maybe they are arriving by spacecraft, we just don't know, but somehow they have heard us and they have come."

At that moment a number of cars suddenly descended upon the Nagaland compound. Many of the cars had red and blue lights flashing. It was the local San Bernardino County sheriffs, the DEA and the MiB.

The Naganites had prepared in case anything like this should happen. Augustus, who was inside the compound near a computer, uploaded the videos to YouTube. He also published the videos on the cult's website.

Within a few hours thousands of people had seen the videos of the Nagas.

-67-

THE RAID

For over an hour it was chaos and pandemonium at Nagaland as various law enforcement officials tried to round up all the people who had come to the drum circle. Several of the Naganites who were in the kitchen area, including Louie and Karina, ran toward the boulders to hide. The officers were less than civil and roughed up a number of people including Bubba, who received several cuts and bruises from being knocked around and dragged across the compound.

Sorting out who was a Naganite and who was a guest took several hours. All the guests were sent home if they seemed sober enough and that included Mitch, Darlene, John, Dylan and Melanie. The sheriff deputies gave Dylan a tough time because of his dreads but eventually let him leave.

Bubba, and all the Naganites who could be found, were forcefully rounded up and arrested, charged with ridiculous crimes, whatever it took to lock them all up. Bubba was especially targeted, he was charged with running a drug operation. Bubba's lawyer, George Maxwell, said that he'd have them all out by sunrise.

The night turned out much different for Louie, Karina and a few other Naganites who had run for it. They quickly found themselves deep in the boulders, lost, surrounded by a dark desert. Louie had used the light from his phone to guide the little group farther into the boulders, away from the sounds of the raid receding in the distance.

After a little while they were in an area where no one had been in a long time. The area was riddled with caves. The group choose a large cave and moved about twenty feet inside. The cave went much farther back into the dark but no one was interested in exploring the depths. They just wanted to hide until the raid was over.

The group settled around the light of the phone and tried to get comfortable. Everyone got quiet and the cave was soon filled with a thick silence, each person lost in their own thoughts and worries about the raid. Louie was especially concerned because he couldn't afford to get arrested, not with his record.

Breaking the silence came a slithering sound from deep in the darkness of the cave. The sound was enough to send the entire group scrambling for the entrance and back out into the night. As the group hid themselves among the boulders, they turned and watched while a dozen Nagas slithered out of the cave.

The Nagas were dressed in fine evening wear, as if they were on their way to an elegant party. The Nagas were mostly males but there were several ladies among the group. All of them had handsome features.

The Nagas seemed to consult together. It looked like a sea of cobras waving in the air over their heads. After a few minutes three of the Nagas headed off into the boulders, towards the compound, while the rest returned to the cave.

Louie, Karina and the others looked at each other in disbelief of what they had seen. Holy shit pretty much summed up their collective feeling at that moment. They stayed hidden in the boulders until the first light of morning. It took several hours before they found their way back to the compound, which was silent and deserted.

It was close to ten in the morning before the Naganites got out of jail. George Maxwell had hired a bus to take them all back to Nagaland.

The pot gardens at Nagaland were gone, destroyed by the DEA, even though all the Ganja was legally grown according to California law. Every part of the compound had been ransacked. Clothes and personal belongings were strewn everywhere. It was obvious that the intention had been to mess up their stuff rather than run a police investigation. Bubba insisted that everyone take photos of the destruction before they cleaned it up.

It took several days before things got back to normal at Nagaland. It would take months to get the pot gardens back to where they were before the raid. Luckily for the Naganites, they had recently stashed ten pounds of Ganja and a couple pounds of hash in a storage unit in Yucca Valley. They still had herb to smoke to get them through until they could grow new crops.

All the charges against Bubba and the Naganites were dropped within a few weeks but the damage had been done. A handful of Naganites left the cult before the month was over. Bubba was devastated by the whole situation and was spending more time alone inside his tepee. Even the word of the new sighting of Nagas did little to lift his spirits.

Louie, Augustus and Randy Rattlesnake went on several excursions into the remote area of the boulders and found the caves but couldn't find any sign of the Nagas. They did find one cave with a passage that seemed to go deep into the recesses of the Earth. They explored as far as they dared and reported back to Bubba. Bubba was more than a little overwhelmed by the raid and had little interest in exploring the cave at the moment.

Melissa Kingsnake held things together while Bubba had a meltdown. Melissa was in love with Bubba and believed one hundred percent in the cult. The cult was her family and she wasn't going to let anything destroy it, not Nagas, not the MiB, not the DEA, not the San Bernardino County sheriffs, nobody.

-68-

AFTER THE RAID

A couple of days later Dylan and Melanie got together for a BBQ with Mitch, Darlene and John.

"What a great view," remarked Darlene after they pulled up at Dylan and Mel's house.

After a brief tour of the house and yard they gathered on the patio overlooking the basin. Quickly the talk turned to the raid a few nights before. None of them knew who had conducted the raid.

"I think it was a DEA raid," said John. "Some of the officers were wearing DEA jackets."

"But why the DEA, why now?" asked Mitch, "These people have been growing and selling pot with a permit since it became legal. It doesn't make much sense."

"How about those guys in the dark suits wearing sunglasses at night?" asked Dylan.

"Yeah, those guys were creepy," said Darlene.

"Way creepy... they had a strange vibe," said Melanie.

"And how about those cops, they were assholes," said Dylan, who still had a bruise on his arm from being handled roughly by the sheriff deputies, "did you see how they treated Bubba?"

"Yeah, they dragged him across the compound. Totally unnecessary. What jerks!" commented John.

After a while the conversation started to drift away from the raid and toward the details of life, you know, stuff like jobs, family, pets, and living situations. Mitch lit up a joint of Bubba Kush and passed it to Dylan as the talk turned to the Lotto.

"No kidding, you really won the Lotto?" asked Dylan, incredulous, taking a big hit and passing the joint to Melanie, "I have never met anyone who won a hundred dollars, let alone a million dollars..."

"Three hundred and twelve million dollars," interjected Mitch, "of course they take over half in taxes."

"Want to buy some art?" joked Melanie, who tried to stifle her cough after taking a hit.

"We might, we just bought a house with five bedrooms and we have lots of walls to fill," replied Darlene, winking at Melanie. Melanie smiled and passed the joint over to Darlene. Darlene took a hit and passed the joint over to John, who took a hit, held it in, exhaled and said, "Ffftzoit".

Meanwhile, on YouTube, the Naganite channel had received millions of hits over the last few days. Interest was extremely high on the videos of the Nagas. The Naganite website was also getting tons of visitors. More than a few of those views were from MiB doing surveillance work.

A number of reporters showed up at Nagaland to check out the story, and the Naganites had to spend several days showing the reporters around the place. Bubba was in no shape for interviews but still he gave about a dozen to various reporters. Bubba was taking the whole event in a deeply personal way and was crushed as individual Naganites started to leave the cult.

The stories written up in the newspapers were invariably negative and sarcastic. No one, it seems, had taken the visit of the Nagas seriously and most reporters thought it was some kind of a hoax. The stories mostly centered on the "strange lifestyle" of the hi-desert cult that grew pot for a living.

-69-

THE NEW HOME

After spending a week in the hi-desert, Mitch, Darlene and John headed back to Long Beach. There was serious moving stuff to take care of now. The house was about a week away from clearing escrow, and Mitch and Darlene were excited to move.

Mitch had to deconstruct his marijuana growing set-up, which took several days. With John's help he got all the pots, lights, growing fertilizers, and all the various paraphernalia into boxes, ready for the movers. Mitch was planning on setting up a new pot grow in one of the greenhouses and was going to grow organic vegetables in the other.

Darlene had flown back to Washington for a few days to pack up some things from her old house. She felt like she stepped into a time warp when she returned home. Everything was where she had left it months earlier, but so much in her life had changed. After several days she realized it was going to take much more time to pack up the little cottage she had lived in for over twenty years. She also missed Mitch, so she flew back to Long Beach, determined to return after they settled into the new house.

Escrow closed near the end of the month. The house was now Mitch and Darlene's. They drove up to Joshua Tree early on a Tuesday to meet Bill Smith at his office and get the keys. The Hopewells brought champagne with them to celebrate, even though they rarely drank. With the keys in their hands they drove out to their new home in North Joshua Tree. They parked Lucky in the RV parking next to the house and walked around the porch. Mitch unlocked the front door and carried Darlene over the threshold. They were home.

The movers were scheduled to bring Mitch's stuff from Long Beach in a few days, so Mitch and Darlene were planning on camping out at their new home while they waited. One day they went and visited Dylan and Mel at the studio. One day they went and bought a new Ford pickup truck at the dealership in Yucca Valley. They realized they needed something besides Lucky to drive around when they weren't traveling.

When Mitch's stuff arrived it barely put a dent into the amount of space they had. It was obvious a home furnishing shopping spree was next on the agenda. They decided on setting up two of the bedrooms as guest rooms, one of them they called John's room. Darlene liked to sew, so they decided to set up a sewing room for her.

"How about we have the house painted?" suggested Mitch after they been there a week. The house was yellow with white trim. "I mean, the house looks fine but I keep thinking how nice it'd look in green with red trim.

"Hmm. Let me think about that," said Darlene. "You don't think it'll look like a Christmas tree do you?"

"No, it'll look great. I did a mock-up on the computer, I'll show you."

They went in the room that was unofficially Mitch's computer room. Mitch had a photo of the front of the house on the screen in a graphics program. He had changed the colors of the house in the photo, it looked pretty cool.

“Oh, that’s what you were doing in here earlier,” said Darlene.

“How do you like the house?” asked Mitch.

“Wow, that really does look great, not like a Christmas tree at all.”

“I was thinking we could have the barn and the garage painted the same colors.”

“Can we have it done while we’re in Washington?”

“That’s what I had in mind. I already called Bill Smith to get the name of a good, local house painter, a guy name Jeremy.”

“Let’s do it,” said Darlene, enthusiastic as usual.

-70-

VISITING BUBBA

Dylan had been watching the Nagaland videos over and over, while making a number of sketches of the Nagas. Dylan didn't doubt for an instant that they were real and that the videos were authentic. He spent a lot of time thinking about what a strange reality we live in, one with strange creatures like these Nagas.

"I think I need to talk to Bubba," said Dylan one morning while he and Mel were sharing the first joint of the day on the patio. "Do you want to come with me?"

"No, I've got a huge list of things I need to do today. You go ahead," said Mel, taking a small hit from the joint.

"Okay, I'm going to head over there soon."

"What do you want to talk to Bubba about?"

"The Nagas. I wonder what he was going to say that night before the raid happened. I keep having Nagas attacking people in my paintings and I need another perspective."

"Why are your Nagas always attacking people?"

"I think I must fear them or something… I'm not really sure. I'm hoping talking to Bubba will help move my thoughts." Dylan took a big hit, exhaled, coughed several times, and said, "Om, Yummie Yummie." He winked at Mel. Imitating

Bubba had become their inside joke.

It was a beautiful day up in Pipes Canyon. The sky was impossibly blue with large white clouds moving rapidly across the sky. The air was especially clear and you could see for miles. Everything had a stunning clarity.

It was just after eleven in the morning when Dylan pulled through the gates at Nagaland. He had worn his Nagas t-shirt, because, you know, he was going to Nagaland. Melissa saw him when he pulled up and walked out to meet him.

"I love that t-shirt," said Melissa as she gave Dylan a hug, "Welcome back to Nagaland."

"Thanks. I came to see Bubba, is he around?" asked Dylan.

"Yeah, he's in his tepee. Let me check if he's seeing anyone today."

"Okay. How are you guys holding up?"

"It's been rough. The cops made a mess of the place and ruined the garden. Some of the members of our group have decided to leave. We're still picking up the pieces. Bubba is taking it especially hard."

"Maybe I came at a bad time?"

"No, let me check with Bubba. Follow me," and she led Dylan into the compound.

She disappeared into Bubba's tepee for a few minutes and then reappeared.

"Bubba will see you in five minutes," said Melissa. "Want to share a joint while you wait? I was just about to have a smoke break."

"Love to," replied Dylan.

Dylan and Melissa found a shady place to sit in the courtyard. Melissa had a joint stuck behind her ear and she lit it up.

"Ffftzoit," said Dylan as he took a hit.

Melissa cracked up and said, "Eyot."

"Here's to the Waldos," said Melissa and she took a hit.

"How long have you lived here?" asked Dylan.

"We've owned the property for several years now, but I've

been following Bubba for seventeen years."

"Do you mind me asking how old you are, because you don't look like you could have been following Bubba for seventeen years?"

"Sure, I'm thirty-nine."

"No way..."

"It's true. I've smoked a lot of Ganja in my time, and Bubba always says that smoking Ganja helps keep you looking and thinking young. I guess that must be true."

"I guess so," replied Dylan, who then changed the subject, "How do things work here at Nagaland? I noticed that Augustus and Sandy were a couple and so are Karina and Louie. Are you guys allowed to have couples in your... group?" He had almost said cult but caught himself at the last second.

"Yes, we have several couples at Nagaland. Unlike many cults, we don't require our members to be single, celibate or anything. Bubba teaches about respect for one another but he doesn't run the member's lives. We're not that kind of cult."

"You don't mind the word *cult?*"

"Oh, not at all. We're not a part of any mainstream religion and we venerate the Nagas, so we're a cult. Most people are afraid of that word but we aren't."

"That's really interesting..." replied Dylan as his mind was starting to drift. It was a really good joint.

"What kind of Ganja is this?" asked Dylan.

"It's a Gorilla Glue strain, or as we call it, Bubba's Glue, mixed with Bubba Kush hash. I should have warned you, it's pretty strong."

"No, no problem. I've got a pretty high tolerance but this joint is really stoning me."

"That's a good thing," said Melissa as she smiled, "Oh, here comes Bubba!"

She passed the joint over to Bubba who took a tremendous hit.

"Om, Yummie Yummie," said Bubba after he exhaled.

"Welcome back to Nagaland," said Bubba as he stuck out his hand and shook Dylan's.

"Thank you," said Dylan, as he brought his hands together over his chest and bowed his head.

"Namaste," said Bubba, as he repeated the gesture.

"Can you tell me about the Nagas?" asked Dylan, "And even more, can you tell me about how you see the world, knowing that you live in a world where Nagas really exist?"

"What can I tell you about the Nagas?" asked Bubba.

"What were you going to say that night at the drum circle before the raid?"

"I was going to talk about the history of the Nagas, you know, Naga 101. Do you need to hear the history of the Nagas?"

"No. I know the history of the Nagas, I've been doing nothing but researching information about these serpent people. I'm an artist, and I keep painting pictures of Nagas attacking people. I was hoping you might help me view the Nagas differently."

"Why are your Nagas attacking people?"

"I really don't know. I thought it might be because I'm afraid of the Nagas, but that idea doesn't satisfy me."

"I don't think that's it. I imagine the Nagas probably represent something to your subconscious, and that's coming out in your paintings."

"Interesting."

"Tell me about your dreams," inquired Bubba, taking a Jungian approach.

Dylan and Bubba ended up talking for several hours about dreams, Carl Jung, the Nagas, consciousness, painting, and life at Nagaland. Little did Dylan know, but Bubba needed this talk more than he did. Bubba hadn't been in the role of a teacher since the Nagas first arrived, and it was good for him to hear himself speaking his ideas out loud. At one point Sandy came by with portobello mushroom burgers for the two of them to eat while they continued talking.

-71-
BACK TO WASHINGTON

Mitch and Darlene drove up to Washington a few weeks later. They were going to pack up all of Darlene's things and have movers bring it down to Joshua Tree. Jeremy was going to paint the house, barn and garage while they were gone.

The trip to Washington was taken at a leisurely pace. The couple took a week to make the drive, stopping in Big Sur, and a few other scenic locations along the way. A few days before they got to Darlene's old home Mitch told Darlene he felt that strange feeling coming on, the feeling he had before his last road rage. Darlene took over the driving for the rest of the afternoon and took them to a KOA campground to stay for a couple of days so Mitch could sleep.

The next day Mitch felt much better and the following day they continued their road trip.

"I think it really helped telling you I had that feeling coming on," said Mitch as they got back on the road.

"You didn't get as sick as last time," replied Darlene, "I definitely believe it helped, you talking about it."

"I'll try and do that in the future."

Their GPS told them they had 176.2 miles to go until Darlene's house. They hoped to get there before noon, so they would have most of the day to pack. The traffic on the road was really bad that morning. Mitch was being extra cautious, several cars had already cut him off. He didn't lose his temper, but it was like the world was trying to push his buttons.

Thankfully, they got to Darlene's house without incident. Everything was as she had left it, a mess of moving supplies. The two assessed the situation and wondered where to begin.

"Let's start in the living room," suggested Darlene, "Then we can stack all the boxes we pack out here."

"First things first," said Mitch, as he got out a joint.

After smoking the joint of a fine Sativa, Mitch and Darlene got to work on packing up the place. After several hours the whole living room was in boxes stacked against one wall, and the furniture was wrapped up for moving, sitting against another wall.

"How about dinner at Harvey's Restaurant, where we met?" suggested Darlene during their next smoke break.

"Harvey's? Was that the name of the place? I'd forgotten," replied Mitch, "Do we need reservations?"

"Nope."

"Then let's do it."

Darlene was remembered fondly at Harvey's, she had been a regular there for years. She introduced Mitch to all her old friends. Some people stopped by their table while they ate to find out what had become of Darlene over the last half a year. Mitch and Darlene told the story of going to Las Vegas to get married, and about their new house in Joshua Tree, again and again. They kept quiet about the whole Lotto thing. They usually kept quiet about the Lotto thing when they first met people, it had a way of tripping most people out.

After dinner the couple continued packing boxes. They were determined to finish up with the sewing room before bed. Of course, they got distracted after smoking another joint. Darlene had so many interesting things she had made over the years: curtains, tablecloths, napkins, embroidered pillows, and clothes. Tons of clothes. Mitch was blown away by the amount of things Darlene had made. He really had no idea Darlene was this creative. When she said she wanted a sewing room he hadn't expected this.

"These will look great in the kitchen," said Mitch, holding up some curtains that had been folded neatly in a box, "You've got so much cool stuff that will look great in the house."

It took two more days, but soon the house was all packed. Mitch called a moving company and made arrangements to have the boxes and furniture moved and they headed back to the hi-desert.

-72-

DYLAN'S BREAKTHROUGH

Dylan's breakthrough with the Nagas and his painting came after a dream. He was paying more attention to his dreams since his talk with Bubba. Dylan dreamed he was a Hindu deity overseeing the Nagas during the creation of the world. He saw the Naga Shesha with the world in his dreaded hair. What he saw looked like a Hindu devotional drawing come to life with Vishnu, Krishna, Kali and many other deities dancing with the Nagas of old. He saw a great Naga protecting the Buddha during a torrential rain shower, his seven cobra heads forming a canopy. The dream was full of visions, and all the visions were about the glory of the Nagas.

"I need to go to the studio right away," said Dylan after his first cup of coffee.

"I saw you drawing like a madman this morning," said Mel.

"Yeah, look at these sketches," said Dylan as he handed her four drawings, several of which had been colored in with pencils.

"Wow, those are some impressive Nagas," said Mel.

"I had a dream last night that was… impressive, and now I have all these images in my head. And none of the Nagas are attacking anyone."

“What made the difference?” asked Mel.

“Veneration. My dream was about the Nagas. When I woke up I realized I needed to venerate the Nagas like the Hindu and the Naganites do.”

“You’re going to paint those on canvas? That should look… *impressive*.” Mel winked as she smiled at Dylan.

The next few days were spent in the studio. Dylan had a vision and he kept riding it. He started with a smaller canvas but quickly moved up in size. These Nagas needed to be worthy of veneration. Mel brought Dylan food and coffee and kept the joints rolled and ready.

A few days in the studio turned into several weeks. Soon Dylan had enough new paintings to call his art dealer in Los Angeles and send her photos of the new work. His art dealer, Monica Berkshire, was ecstatic over Dylan’s new work and said she would have five of the paintings sold before the end of the week.

Dylan got off the phone with Monica, and gave Mel the thumbs up. Mel handed Dylan a joint and he lit it up.

“Ffftzoit,” said Dylan as he took a hit.

-73-

SMOKE BREAK

This is our last smoke break before we wrap up this story. I really appreciate you reading my little novel. Before I go I want to talk a little bit about the relationship we form with the herb.

A relationship with the herb is like many relationships you form in life. The high you get from the relationship is something that changes over a long period of time. The early marijuana experience is so much different than the thirty or thirty-five year experience.

I've been smoking the herb for nearly thirty-five years. I've quit for periods of time, or taken breaks from the herb but never with the intention of leaving for good. It's good to take a break from Mary Jane every once in a while, if for no other reason than to reflect on your relationship with the plant. But I always come back because this is what makes me feel right.

I've found that most people who experience life with a bipolar disorder or severe depression often use marijuana to make themselves feel right. I don't think there is anything wrong with that.

My body has always felt uncomfortable. Often I've described how I felt before I discovered marijuana was that my spirit didn't quite seem to fit into my body, like a square peg in a round hole. That changed the day I first smoked pot. Like Dylan in this story, I felt right from the first time smoking the herb. That is one of the reasons I have smoked all these years. Most everything about my relationship with the herb has changed over the years, but not how it makes my body feel.

Sometimes I miss the early days when getting stoned tripped me out. In the early days of the pot relationship everything trips a person out, and it's often hysterically funny, at least to them. Later they start to get used to the relationship and it's not so trippy. They start to experience other aspects of the marijuana high. After about three years, if the person is still smoking pot, they are probably questioning the relationship, and wondering if it's working out. Most people quit pot around three years into smoking it. I read a study about this years ago. A small portion of people who start smoking pot, keep smoking after three years. Those people tend to become pot smokers for life.

Many people end up having an "on again, off again," relationship with pot. They smoke pot for a while, and really love it, but drift away from smoking herb for a number of reasons: job, relationship, school, etc.. Later, under some kind of circumstance, like Louie in our story, the opportunity to take a couple hits of pot comes up for the first time in years and they have a smoke. The smoking experience is great, and they remember for a moment how great pot was, but the next day they get back to their regularly scheduled life. This is the kind of relationship most people develop with the herb.

I wish I could say smoking herb is great and wonderful for everyone but that's not the truth. Some people just don't do well with the herb. It overwhelms their senses and leaves them feeling disoriented. This is a small percentage of the population and of the many, many people I've smoked with over the years only two have had adverse reactions.

Smoking the herb will change you over time and I think that's a good thing. Bubba Ravi Shesha was right when he said that smoking the herb will keep you thinking and looking young. Smoking herb will alter a person's sense of speed moving through the world and tends to slow people down, thank goodness. We move far to quickly through this life and it would benefit many people to slow down for a while and just move at the speed of time.

One last thing I wanted to say about pot smoking, that I forgot to mention earlier, is about set and setting.

There are many factors that will influence your pot smoking experience, the main factor being the kind of herb a person is smoking. The other major factors include something called set and setting.

Set is about a person's mindset. Marijuana tends to be an intensifier, so whatever the mindset is going into smoking pot will affect a person's high. I smoke pot to help alleviate the symptoms of depression, so I go into my high with the mindset that this is going to help relieve my symptoms. My mindset is on healing and health. When I smoke pot recreationally I have my mind on kicking back and relaxing. I get myself ready to enjoy the high.

Setting refers to the place, the location where a person is getting high. Is it a good place to smoke some herb? Will they be able to relax, or is it an environment that will lead to high anxiety? Choose your smoking places wisely because it will have a huge impact on the high you experience.

Okay, that's it, back to the conclusion of our story.

-74-

THE ROAD BACK

After a few months Bubba was starting to get his groove back. Talking with Dylan had gotten him thinking again, and now he was seeing a path forward. He resumed his spiritual teacher role. "Every teacher is a student, every student is a teacher," became one of his new maxims. He was no longer shaken up by the reality of the Nagas. He had come to terms with that. He was now at the point where he was glad he had gone through his moment of doubt.

Bubba took up the role of spiritual teacher with renewed vigor. The moment of doubt had strengthened many of Bubba core ideas and had shaken loose a few of the flakier ones. Bubba still believed he was the reincarnation of the first discoverer of Ganja, he still believed in the Nommos, and he definitely believed in the Nagas.

Louie, Tony and the Naganites replanted the garden, and the first new Ganja plants were nearly ready to be harvested. The Naganites who had decided to stay had bonded tighter as a group, more determined than ever, not only to survive, but to thrive.

It took a little while but soon the cult started to thrive again.

Louie and Tony brought the garden back to full capacity. Louie started working on developing a new strain called Oro Bud. Karina joined the cult and took Louie's last name though everyone still calls her Fire Dreamer. Louie and Karina were expecting a child soon. Louie no longer smells like prison to himself.

Melissa and Bubba finally, after all these years, admitted they were in love and did something about it; Melissa moved into Bubba's tepee. Nine months later Bubba Jr. was born.

More people came and joined their little social experiment. The drum circles continued every new moon and full moon. Melissa eventually convinced Bubba that they needed a gift shop, so finally they have one. It does pretty good business selling Naga Bars, Dylan's t-shirts, several strains of premium Ganja and various art works created by Naganites.

The Nagas, well, they stayed underground and didn't return again. As a matter of fact, they closed up the entrance to the underground from inside. It will be centuries, and in another story, before the entrance will be opened and humans and Nagas will finally be able to meet.

The Nommos found Joshua Tree to be getting a bit too crowded to spend much time there. Lots of people saw their spaceship as it flew around the sky above the National Park. The Nommos are now on their way back to Sirius, taking their bad report with them.

-75-

FFFTZOIT

A year has passed since the raid on Nagaland. Dylan and Mel have become great friends with Mitch and Darlene. So far the Hopewells have bought four of Dylan's paintings of the Nagas. The new house looks great in green and red. John has been coming up to visit often. He's still thinking about moving to the hi-desert.

Mitch and Darlene now have two dogs, a Jack Russell named Obie and a rat terrier named Biscuit. John loves playing with Obie and Biscuit when he visits. Darlene is thinking about getting a miniature horse or two.

Augustus and Sandy got married in a traditional Naganite ceremony officiated by Bubba, of course. Little Bubba Jr. is crawling around but not walking yet. He's going to have an interesting life, take my word for it. Many years later he will become a conservative lawyer.

Melissa and Bubba lived together for many more years and watched their cult grow until there were 45 Naganites living at Nagaland. The social experiment was working out all right.

The Earth, this little blue and green ball, is still corkscrewing through the galaxy at 514,000 mph, and will for the foreseeable future, moving at the speed of time. The good news is that the planet is just about out of this bad section of galaxy we've been in for thousands of years, so things should be looking up soon.

Meanwhile, the herb is still illegal in far too many places, for far too many ridiculous reasons. In the future, I imagine it'll become more and more normalized, more legal. I certainly hope so. Drug prohibition is just one of the symptoms of the Kali Yuga, so, like I've said, that should be changing soon.

As a way of bringing this story in for a landing I'd like to remind you of this important point: *I am consciousness having the experience of being me. You are consciousness having the experience of being you. We are made of the same cloud of dust, living in a world of illusions. We are energy, information and all possibilities.*

Ffftzoit!

P.S. I have just enough pot left to roll up one last joint. Seeing as it's now 4:20 in the morning, I think I'll light it up and send out my stoned vibes to the world. Eyot 420 :)

JON CHRISTOPHER was born and raised in Southern California. He lives with his love of more than 30 years, Tania, in the hi-desert overlooking Joshua Tree National Park. Jon's either writing, creating music, painting or designing books for Traveling Shoes Press – and always spending time with Suki the dog.

ALSO BY JON CHRISTOPHER

"I laughed out-loud reading this book. Very entertaining… delivered in a style that says 'You're in on the secret.'"
– Michael Whyte, a really great cook in Hailey Idaho

"Jon Christopher's amazing debut novel is a clever synthesis of situations connected to an anything-is-possible and otherworld plot line…which is at once fast-paced, surprisingly metaphysical, and undeniably clever."
– Mark Leysen, author of *The Klown*, Irvine California

"William S. Burroughs meets X-Files inspired mind-twisting fiction."
– Adrienne Linn, Paramedic in Yuciapa California

SOMEWHERE.TRAVELINGSHOESPRESS.COM

Ffftzoit!

www.ingramcontent.com/pod-product-compliance
Lightning Source LLC
Chambersburg PA
CBHW020936310726
48980CB00007B/802/J

* 9 7 8 1 7 3 2 9 2 0 5 6 9 *